EVANESCENT

THE SEMPITERNAL SERIES

BOOK ONE

By

Sara V. Zook and Wendy S. Chartier

PLANETTOPIA PUBLISHING

Evanescent

Planettopia Publishing LLC

©2014 Sara V. Zook and Wendy S. Chartier

EBook:

ISBN-10: 1941246915

ISBN- 13: 978-1-941246-91-7

Print:

ISBN-10: 1941246923

ISBN-13: 978-1-941246-92-4

Dedication
-Wendy-

This book is dedicated to my husband, David Chartier.
Thank you for all the love and encouragement.
Without you, Sarenah and Draco would not exist.
You are my Draco!
And yes, I would fight Heaven and Hell for you.

To my mom Charlotte and sister Rebecca.
I love you both more than you will ever know.

Nancy Bowers Roberts, you were a huge part of my
growing up years and I thank you for some of the
best memories of my life. I love you!

A huge thank you to author Sara V. Zook. You are a
talented writer and a great friend.
I never could have done this without you.
To many more adventures!
M...G...R!
Author Karen Luellen, thank you for your friendship
and encouragement. You are the best!

Panda <3 Penguin

Author Renee Cleveland. You have been my best friend for many years and I love you dearly. Thank you for all your love and encouragement, Lil'bit!

William Elmore you will always be PRFTSAINT to me, therefore in many ways you are Saint. Thank you for being who you are, an honest, and no BS kind of guy.
Love Me

And a special thank you to Aly, wherever you are.

Dedication

-Sara-

I dedicate this book to Wendy. Thank you for entrusting me with putting your vision into words. I am so grateful to have you as my friend, publisher and co-author. M. G. R.!

I would like to thank everyone who helped make Book 1 in the The Sempiternal Series a reality. There were many late nights in writing this one and probably too many fast food meals. To my family and friends who listened to me shoot around ideas, a huge thanks. Stefanie Fontecha with Beetiful Graphic Designs, your covers rock, and this one is no exception.

To my readers, I hope you thoroughly enjoy this one. Your support means everything.

- Sara V. Zook –

Run fast, run furious to the arms you trust the most
and hold you tightest.
-David Chartier

Evanescent

Prologue

Panic surged through me. I looked up and saw the intensity in everyone's eyes as we just stood frozen in time, no one daring to move, breathe, yet each of us felt it coming as the storm brewed underneath us.

A shadow crept upon the Heavens, its darkness growing by the moment as the eternal illumination that we called home seemed as if it were slowly being snuffed out.

I sucked in a breath and almost gagged. I knew they'd be upon us soon, their stench like the decay of a thousand rotting bodies filling my nostrils, making me almost retch. My fingers slid across the smooth handle of my sword, waiting, my entire body ready to launch at any given moment.

Why? Why would they be trying to attack us knowing they had no chance? They had no hope.

Thoughts raced through my mind that there had to be a reason, one unknown to the rest of us. A dizzy sensation coursed through me as my mind and emotions melded together.

Were the rest of them thinking the same as me? Surely, they were. I could see the flames in their eyes, ready, willing, with a hint of terror.

I tried to shake it all from my head. It didn't matter what the reason. We *would* defend ourselves and our hope. We were soldiers of the light. Victory would reign, and that victory would be ours.

The shadow became more apparent, and the noise of a muffled buzzing grew louder, stronger.

They weren't far off now. Would they be able to break through?

Movement caught my eye. I looked up to see one of our own. Her wings shook free and fluttered about. She quickly tucked them back in again, lowering her eyes in shame as the tremors took over her body. Disgust emanated from within me. She had always been weak. She should just run away, the coward.

The buzzing increased and had switched over to a grinding sound of bone on bone.

A thunderous noise echoed throughout the Heavens. The ground shook. I almost lost my balance but somehow managed to stay upright. Others fell down all around me.

They were here.

Another horrific blow of all their weight pushing against our ground. Even I couldn't help but fall.

Quickly jumping to my feet, I wrapped my fingers around my sword and pulled it from its heavy sheath. My heart pounded wildly, my chest heaving as the adrenaline coursed through my veins.

What was happening?

There was no more movement, no more noise. The silence was piercing through us all. It was agonizing and sweet all at the same time. We were ready to launch, yet nothing was happening. Had they figured out they couldn't enter?

I saw everyone's eyes fill with relief.

No, no, not yet. It's a trick. It has to be a trick. They've come all this way and know they'll be killed if they fail their mission. They're replaceable, always someone more than willing to take their place. They know this. They're not stupid. It's foolish to think they're going to leave.

The shadow was still there, but why wasn't there any noise?

4

Then the buzzing and grinding pulsated through the Heavens. The noise seemed to be in one particular spot. Those that were standing over it backed away, the uncertainty of the situation too much to bear.

The noise changed again to scratching. It was fast and precise.

"What's going on?" someone asked.

They're clawing their way in, I just know it. They're trying to make a hole, but they can't. It's not possible. My thoughts wavered in my mind. *They can't, but they're trying, and knowing they can't can only mean that they possibly could...*why would this be allowed?

My concentration was thrown off from the task at hand. *If they* do, *they* will *be destroyed.* We were immortal soldiers. The *what-ifs* could be saved for later.

A shriek sounded.

I was not alone in my distress.

A single hand with decaying flesh and curled black nails appeared through the surface of the

Heavens. It was like a hallucination as we all stared, disbelieving such a thing could be a reality.

They were here. The demons had made their way to us, to our home.

My grasp on my sword tightened as the little entrance one demon had made turned into a massive hole of hundreds upon hundreds of their reeking, dark forms pouring into the one place we had always assumed safe.

I had never seen such a creature up close before. They were even more horrific than I'd ever imagined, with glowing red, green, and yellow eyes and gnashing teeth.

Metal connected with bone as our swords collided with their extremities. They didn't even attempt to protect themselves. They just came at us with their arms and mouths, trying to tear us to shreds with their claws and teeth.

I lifted my sword up high and swung down as it tore through one of the creature's necks. It made an eerie screeching sound as it shriveled into nothing but a pile of black dust on the floor of the Heavens.

A hot liquid splashed across my face. I wiped it with the back of my hand, my tongue tasting the blood of the angel at my side as one of the creatures ferociously feasted on his neck.

I spit, trying to remove the disgusting taste, and lifted my sword up. It came down on the dark creature's back, and again it squealed and trembled until it dissolved into nothingness. I examined the face of the angel on the ground who now lay motionless. Dead? Could it be? But this was a place of life.

A large, dark creature made its way through the hole in the midst of the chaos. All around me angels were fighting with the demons. The creature was hidden by a red cape and hood so no one could see its true form.

I couldn't take my eyes away from it. Another demon attacked me. I quickly slew it as it lay in a pile beside the other one I had killed.

This creature...this was the demon's master. Something terrible was going on.

An arm lifted from the cape as long, bony fingers extended and a single finger pointed out toward me.

7

"That one," a deep voice mumbled. "That one is the one I want."

I looked around at the other angels, but the war was still raging around me.

Me? Did he mean me? I looked behind me, not seeing anyone else. *This doesn't look good.*

My sword slipped from my fingers and fell to the ground. Demonic figures leapt onto me, but they didn't gnaw or attempt to kill me. One hung from my right hand, another from my left, and still another jumped onto my back so I'd collapse to the ground.

I looked up at the large, disguised creature. It lowered its hand which disappeared back into the cape.

"Bring her to me."

1

Sarenah

Sparks danced up into the night air as another section of the house burst into flames. Sirens blared in the distance. I sat with my head in my palm at the top of a tree, looking down.

The wind picked up and the fire spread. Screams came from inside the house.

I tapped the side of my face as more sparks shot upward past my head. So beautiful were these little beams of light amongst such tragedy that was occurring before my very eyes. I wanted to reach out and touch the sparks, let them linger on my fingertips.

A tanker pulled into the driveway as a coughing female exited the home. An ambulance came next, its flashing lights spotlighting the woods next to the house. Paramedics jumped out of the vehicle and hurried toward the female.

The very way his body moved when he walked had made my chest tighten. I looked up and our eyes met. For an instant, he stopped moving, his stare burning into the very pit of my being. One of my wings almost flopped down because this creature had

10

taken me by surprise, but I remained in control of myself.

I had run into creatures of the dark before. We merely ignored one another's presence and kept going about what it was we were supposed to do. This time had been different. This creature's magnetic force drew me in.

He was unlike any demonic form I had known to exist. He was tall, muscular, with long, dark hair...almost man-like. His eyes were mesmerizing. His sly smile drew me in even more.

A loud explosion echoed into the darkness followed by an enormous cloud of gray smoke. The female cried out as firemen kicked down the side door of the house and entered.

More firemen clamped their hands upon a huge hose as the water squirted upward and then down, trying to quiet the flames. The roof of the house crackled from the intensity of the fire.

A male child was tossed down from one of the upstairs windows and into the arms of a fireman standing below. His mother rushed over to him and swooped him up in her arms, but the paramedics pried the coughing child from the grips of the hysterical mother and took him to their vehicle to examine him.

The dark creature walked over to me, unusually close, the heat from his skin leaping onto mine. He held up his open palm. As if entranced, I placed my hand upon his and our fingers laced together. Suddenly the darkness of his eyes was illuminated with swirls of hypnotic colors circling each other in the very middle where his pupils should be.

I knew I shouldn't be here, shouldn't be touching this sinful creature, but I couldn't stop. His touch was hot with a passion I had never known before, yet so familiar. I was caught in a trap that I never wanted to get out of.

His other hand dug into my hair and jerked my head back, his breath hot on my neck, his eyes peering into mine.

"How many more, ma'am?" a fireman shouted out above the sirens.

The female just stood there in front of the smoldering shelter before her, both hands covering her face, ashen-filled tears falling from the edge of her jaw.

"Ma'am!" the fireman hollered out. "Who else are you missing?"

The wind changed directions. I looked up to see another angel passing by, carrying the breeze along with her. She raised her hand ever so slightly to wave. I nodded at her.

The fireman covered his nostrils with the inside of his arm as the wind carried the sultry smoke toward him.

The female seemed unaffected by the smoke. She just kept staring at that front door, her apprehension more of a focus now as she waited. "Two," she finally replied.

"Did she say two?" another guy asked.

"Two?" he asked her again to confirm.

Never looking his way, she nodded. "My husband, he went back in for our oldest son."

"Who are you?" I whispered, my chest heaving up and down from his firm grasp on my hair. My anger flared. I should kill him for putting his hands on me like that, but it felt so good.

13

He narrowed his eyes at me for a moment before answering, "Draco."

Draco.

He released me as I stood up straight, facing him. I knew who this strange creature was. I had heard about him on my travels. He was a solider of the dark, with strength witnesses marveled at. Most of the soldiers of the dark were cowards who slithered here and there with little, if any, common sense about their purpose or duty at hand. It was said that this Draco's loyalty surpassed all others. But there was one other tidbit I had heard that was even more unusual. Those who worked with him, who were on the same side, seemed to like him. It was a concept unheard of for the dark side. Everyone was your enemy and everyone hated each other.

"And you are?" he asked.

If I said my name, he'd know who I was as well, and he'd run away. My intrigue was far too deep to have him disappear just yet.

"It doesn't matter, does it?" I said.

He smirked, a dimple forming in the side of his cheek.

What the heck was wrong with me? I wanted to run my fingers over his lips. I should've reigned in those thoughts faster! I had urged myself to try to focus on what was happening around me, not to look at him.

Part of the roof began to sink, until finally caving in with a horrific crushing noise. This caused another flame to appear in a new section, the orange and blue colors lapping up all the oxygen around them.

The female was still standing in front of the door. I looked at my fingernail. A male child cried out from the door of the ambulance, the noise terrifying the poor thing.

"Get Jeff out of there!" a fireman shouted as he fumbled to remove his walkie-talkie from his belt. He pushed a button down on the side of the small device. "Jeff, can you hear me? Jeff, are you okay? Jeff, get out! Get out of there now!"

Another siren echoed in the distance attached to another tanker. I frowned and looked up at the stars dotting the skyline. I felt my mind drifting to him again.

He took a step closer to me. I backed up. Amusement danced in those eyes of his. He reached out; I moved back another step.

"Surely, you're not afraid of me?"

Forbidden was more like the term that came to mind. We weren't to interact with creatures of the dark, and likewise, they with us.

I knew I should reveal to him my name, but I didn't want to. I wasn't thinking clearly. My head seemed to be filled with fog. I told myself to pull it together. I was a warrior angel, not some addle-minded girl.

I wondered why he didn't at least take me as a creature of the light. Couldn't he sense the light? Perhaps it was my enormous wings the color of coal tucked in securely to my back. They always gave me the appearance of being a darker shade than the other angels. I could only make the assumption that this Draco took me as one of his own.

His hands grabbed onto my waist and pulled me forward into his chest.

"Draco...no," I whispered, but in my head I was saying *yes.*

16

"Say it again," he pleaded, his lips gliding across the top of my forehead as he spoke.

The energy I felt being next to him was unlike anything I had ever experienced before. It engulfed every inch of me.

"Say what?" I asked, completely aware of how close our faces were.

He chuckled, and, my hands pressed against his chest, I felt the noise radiating through him.

"My name."

I looked up at his face, his square jaw, and his stormy eyes. My lips parted and with a smirk I said, "No."

A growling noise escaped from his throat. He narrowed his eyes, his hands around my waist pressing me tighter into his body.

"You dare defy me?" he whispered.

I stared back with my left eyebrow arched, not allowing my eyes to turn away from him, so he knew his intimidation couldn't make me cower.

"You're not afraid?" He inspected every inch of my face as if memorizing each feature.

My body tingled from the overwhelming emotions. I had never felt this strange before. There was an ache in the pit of my stomach and a comfort in staring in this dark creature's eyes as if he had put me under some sort of spell.

I reached up and let my fingertip trace the edge of his bottom lip. I grinned.

The female gasped as she saw the front door broken apart from the inside. Smoke poured out from the inflamed house, its beams and foundation creaking and on the brink of crumpling completely down.

Out came the fireman, a small child in his arms. She rushed to him. The firefighter handed him over and then fell to one knee on the ground.

The medics came to attend to the male child, his face covered in soot, his dark eyes huge at the scene before him.

"It's okay, ma'am!" the medic yelled out. "We got him! He needs oxygen!"

The medic had to practically pull the child out of his mother's arms. As he did, she drew her fingers into her mouth, her moist eyes returning to the fireman who was still kneeling down.

"Jeff, you okay?" another fireman asked him. He tried to help him up by putting his arm underneath him, but the man they called Jeff swatted him away.

"No, I got to go back in."

"What? You can't! That whole thing is ready to fall."

Jeff stood up then and put his mask back on. "He was right behind me. He's got to be right there." His eyes met the female's as he headed back to the front door.

Draco withdrew from my touch for a moment, his eyes turning from anger to astonishment.

"What are you doing?" he asked.

The corners of my mouth lifted upward in a small smile. "You feel it, too, don't you?"

I could feel his heart hammering away in his chest, a vein protruding from his neck where a scar lay.

"I..." he mumbled, searching my eyes for an explanation for this intensity.

19

"You can't let go of me, can you?" I asked, my hand running through his black hair.

For a few moments more he studied me, but this time he didn't pull away from my touch. He leaned in and pressed his lips against mine. As if I didn't think the emotions could grow any stronger. My head was spinning in a thousand different directions. This was wrong but felt so right. He kissed me gently, and then I kissed back harder as if trying to melt into him, but it was impossible to get any closer than we already were. My entire body felt alive, every nerve ending inflamed, the heat coursing through my veins. I felt so consumed by Draco. I couldn't breathe, and I loved every second of it.

A stinging pain etched its way to a spot near where my wing attached to my back. I pulled away from Draco quickly, my hand releasing hold on him and trying to find the newly-formed wound.

"What's wrong?" he asked, his eyes on me, his arms still extended as I backed further away, the pain feeling as if one part of my skin was on fire.

It started to ease a little, but I couldn't see what had happened to me. I felt exhilarated, exhausted, and guilty all at the same time.

"Are you okay?"

Was he concerned for me? I watched him take a few steps toward me, his large, strong body moving in that rhythmic and enticing way.

"I...think so. Something's hurting on my back," I quickly explained.

His eyebrows lowered. He was concerned. A creature of the dark didn't care about anything or anyone but themselves. He was a walking contradiction.

"Let me see," he said, trying to look behind me.

Afraid he'd see my wings, I turned so I was facing him again. "I'm fine," I snapped.

His eyes grew large, something stewing within them again as if trying to read my thoughts.

"Who are you?" he asked, the distance between us minimal, his hands up as if ready to dive back into what we had just been doing in an instant, but he was being careful. He didn't want me to run away.

"I can't tell you," I said, my voice crackling under the desire to leap back into his arms, the burning still lingering on my back.

"Okay." He lowered his hands. "What are you?"

I felt a tremendous pull on my heart. I took a step closer to Draco. His hand automatically weaved its way into mine.

"Whatever you are," he continued, "you're beautiful, and I'm drawn to you in a way I can't even explain."

I looked from his eyes to his lips, feeling the exact same way.

He pulled me close again, his lips gliding across mine.

I jumped back, the same unknown burning sensation in my back again.

He looked confused.

"I'm sorry," I said. "Something's wrong."

"What could possibly be wrong?" he asked, his expression one of utter rejection.

My heart was slamming against my ribs. The burning subsided the farther away I was from him. I took a few more steps backward. It felt even better. I

22

wished I could see behind me to know what was going on, where this pain had erupted from.

"I have to go," I told him.

He raised his arm up as if trying to hang on. "Please, no. Don't leave yet. I don't even know who you are..."

"It doesn't matter," I called out, putting more distance between us so that I couldn't see the twisted emotions in his eyes any longer. "This can't happen again, won't happen again."

With that, I turned and ran until completely out of Draco's sight, at which time I spread my wings and launched into the sky.

Movement shifted from behind the jagged edges of the broken front door. The fireman named Jeff came out again, dragging behind him an adult male. He was limp as the other fireman rushed over to help pull him into the middle of the yard, away from the grasps of the choking smoke and growing flames.

Another tanker made its way into the driveway and next to the house followed by police cars. The men poured out of their vehicles and hurried to make strides at quieting the blazing fire.

It was a mess of chaos with the bright, blinking lights, the collapsing of the house, and loud voices hollering out commands in the dark night. Medics rushed to the aid of the adult male. I kept my eyes on him, waiting for my moment. The female fell to all fours on the damp ground and watched in horror as the medics began CPR. Her shrieks were louder than all the rest.

Another angel came and landed on the branches of another tree across from me. Our eyes met. I was a little annoyed at the sight of him. He had just been passing through. He should just keep going and leave me be.

I glanced down at the adult male human again. He was lifeless as they frantically worked to bring him back.

I swooped down next to the male. I studied his face, black streaks speckling his pale skin. The female continued to cry out. I watched her curiously. She loved him with every inch of her being as she saw him slipping out of her grasp. It was amazing really how the reality of losing something could take hold of someone that fiercely. Tragedy showed mercy for no one.

I looked back to the male, the serenity of his closed eyes. I placed my hand on his chest. His eyes instantly snapped open. He looked up at me as if truly seeing me. I took hold of his hand and bent down, placing a kiss upon his sweaty forehead. Then I let go of him and stood, waiting, watching.

"We have a pulse!" a medic cried out.

They placed the oxygen mask over his face as more people brought over a board to carry him on. They transported him to the back of the ambulance. The adult male reached his hand toward the female as he passed nearby her. She, too, reached out and clutched onto it.

I watched them for a moment longer. The angel above me launched and left the scene. I took a giant leap into the darkness above me as the entire house collapsed down below.

2

Draco

"What do you think you're doing?" I yelled out.

The shadows were mute as they all jumped on me to bring me to the ground. I shook one of them free from my arm but another took hold of me. There were just too many of them as I struggled, unable to move as another one landed on the back of my head. My face was forced into the soggy ground beneath me. I tried to suck in a breath as the wet clumps of dirt wedged their way into my nostrils.

They pulled me backwards, and it took almost ten of them to get me to my feet. My hands were bound behind my back. I spit the dirt from my mouth, the fury growing within me.

"How dare you do this to me!" I screamed at them. "You'd better hope I don't break free from these restraints," I threatened.

A collar made of titanium was attached to my neck. I swallowed, my Adam's apple hitting the collar, making the sensation of suffocation creep over me. Then a titanium chain was attached to the front and more shadows hurried to grab onto the chain. They pulled me forward like a hellhound.

My feet were forced to walk onward. Where we were headed, I had no clue. I searched my mind for any indication as to what I may have done to deserve such shameful captivity, but I found no answer to the questions swimming around in my mind.

An enormous metal door opened in front of me. The shadows seemed as if they were floating effortlessly on top of the ground, each one of them swaying in a different direction, their forms never seeming to take on one particular shape for more than a few seconds.

We were not going in there, were we? I hadn't been beyond this door before, but I had seen it, and I knew that once behind it, I'd be in trouble.

I may have been powerful before, possibly the one with the highest rank, but here I'd be made into a mole.

Fear tried to make its way up from the pit of my stomach. I clenched my teeth together and attempted to swallow it back down. Surely this was some kind of test. I had done nothing disloyal.

The farther I was dragged down into the depths of this hell, the more worry took over. I passed cage after cage of lost creatures being held captive, being tortured with the worst kind of torment imaginable, that creature's worst fear.

There had been light at first, but not here, not where I was going. A bead of sweat made its way down the side of my face. It was a combination of the extreme heat versus my own anxiety.

I saw a pool of darkness ahead. It seemed that the light just stopped and there was nothingness. I cringed when I realized this wasn't a test. This was real. Something was terribly wrong, and I was the one being punished this time. I was going to be inside one of these cages, locked in with my worst fear. The realization made me stop dead in my tracks.

The shadows that had been holding onto the chain fell backwards, although I could barely make them out anymore as they began to mix in with the black in front of me.

"No," I said sternly, trying to sound as if I still had my wits about me. "I'm not taking another step."

The little, silent creatures pulled with all their strength until I was down on the ground again. They jumped on me again like vultures, pulling on the skin

29

on the back of my arms as they attempted to force me back into a standing position. *Well, the little bastards will have to drag me, then.*

This went on for a few minutes longer before someone came up behind me. I could feel his presence as he carried a cool draft of wind along with him. It felt good in comparison to the heat that had been gnawing at my skin moments earlier.

"Draco, what is this?"

I looked up into the face of Tuliak. He was one of the oldest and most experienced guards and someone I genuinely respected. His head was bald, but he had a long, flowing gray beard that reached to his waist.

"I'm not going down there," I replied.

Tuliak shook his hands in the air, motioning for the shadows to leave. They made little squealing noises as they ran off.

"Get up, Draco," he ordered.

It was more difficult a task with my hands still bound tightly behind my back.

Tuliak examined me for a moment. "This is nonsense. You *are* going to go down there and take what you rightfully deserve."

The fury took over again, followed by pangs of anxiety. The combination of it sent a course of numbness throughout every fiber of my being.

"I don't deserve to be here. What the fuck did I do wrong?" I snapped.

Tuliak raised his hand and shook his finger at me as though chastising a child. "Now, now, Draco, you and I both know that not to be true. You wouldn't be headed in this direction if that were so."

"I'm telling you, Tuliak, I've been nothing short of loyal..."

"I don't want to hear your excuses," he stated, cutting me off. "Come with me."

I'd been on my own for years doing odd jobs here and there. I had gained my own respect even in the depths of this pit of hell, and yet here I was, my hands were tied, a chain was still dangling from my neck, and I didn't even comprehend why. *At least give me the satisfaction of a reason.*

I followed Tuliak until there was no way of seeing anymore, and I was sure if he stopped, I'd run straight into him. Then I heard the sound of a heavy cage door opening. *My cage.*

31

There was a tug on my chain as Tuliak now had control over it.

"I believe this is where you belong," he said, his voice seeming to echo off the walls as if we were the only two creatures in this whole entire area.

He gave the chain a greater pull and I was forced to go inside. I stood there for a few seconds listening as the door shut again. I didn't move a muscle.

"You must have some things to think over," Tuliak said. "Perhaps try thinking them over before the terror gets into your head and you can't think straight anymore." He chuckled as I heard him walking away from me.

I searched my thoughts for what I was to do. I could feel no chair, no nothing. All around me was blackness, a deafening silence.

I knew this area was saved particularly for the worst kind of torture, and that your worst fear would be played out before you. I could feel the claustrophobia getting to me already. My breath quickened. This kind of evil was saved for those who were especially strong, someone who fit the

32

description of me. They were trying to break me, see how far I could be pushed.

"I don't belong here!" I cried out, my words echoing into the nothingness. "I did nothing wrong!"

I listened to the silence replying to my outburst. Silence. Darkness. That was my worst fear. I couldn't even see my hand in front of me. The madness was already creeping in. I had to find a place in my head that could save me from this wretched torment. I had to find sanctuary, and fast.

I closed my eyes, pretending that the darkness was only there because I was resting and not because it was caving in on me. I sat down on the cold floor beneath me. I immediately reached for the collar around my neck and found it was unlatched; I yanked it from my body and the chain binding my wrists fell away.

With my eyes still shut tightly, I got up and walked forward until I ran into the door of the cage. I pushed on it. It creaked slightly but no movement. I tried again and again, even trying to pry the bars apart, until blood seeped from my body from slamming against the metal. It was no use. There was no escape.

I returned to the middle of the floor and sat back down. I tried to control my breathing. It felt as though the walls were becoming closer together with each passing moment. The silence pierced through my ears, causing more sweat to appear on my brow. My body throbbed from the pain I had just inflicted upon myself. All of my senses were heightened at the fact that this could be my eternal home.

Oh, how I wished for my MP3 player. *How will I survive without my music?* Music kept me sane most of the time. *That's okay, they can try to break me, but I have music in my head that will do just fine.*

I brought my fingers to my lips and let my thoughts drift back to one of the strangest moments I had ever encountered. I closed my eyes and could still see her face, those enticing lips. And her smell... *Who is she?* A part of me felt as if I knew her. Why? Her long hair fell to her hips, the color of a raven.

Her...who was she?

I desperately needed to know her name. If ever I managed to get out of this black hole, I would search Heaven, Hell and everywhere in between to find her.

3

Sarenah

I swooped down to the open window and hesitated before entering the house. Voices were already rising, the male's tone one of degrade, the woman's one of lost hope.

It was a large colonial home with no children to fill it. It looked picture perfect from the outside, but inside was another story. The inside had been subjected to their fights on many occasions, and even more so of late. It was where the storm brewed.

This day was unlike all the rest. The basis of where their outbursts were coming from was the same as always.

Draco's face appeared in my head again. His lips had been so close to mine as he spoke.

I shook the memory from my mind and went in through the window, bringing a small breeze along with me that rustled the sheer curtains.

"You keep saying that over and over!" the female yelled. "Nothing is ever going to change. Nothing ever does with you!"

"This is all your fault! If I had to do it all over again..."

"You'd what? Tell me! Just say it!"

The male wrinkled his face at her in disgust. "I'd have married Laura."

The female's anger rose. "Go to hell! I hate you!"

Their battle went on.

I stood in the corner, patiently waiting, wondering why it was that people who thought themselves in love could wrestle with each other's emotions in this way. It didn't seem right that they could ruin each other like this. If only they could see how short the life of a human actually was, perhaps they'd change their minds about the constant bickering that wasted away their hours and their energy.

My thoughts drifted to Draco again, his lips pressed against mine. He was so beautiful, chiseled and broad. I still couldn't get my head wrapped around what exactly had happened between the two of us. It was insane, really. Angels did not interfere with the motions of the dark creatures and vice versa. It was forbidden, unheard of, and truly, they were all very ugly, sickly-looking things. That is, until Draco appeared. He had a mesmerizing grip on me, even now as I couldn't help myself but to continue to think of him, long for him. I had never experienced anything like this before.

The guilt was still there, plaguing me. Draco would appear in my mind followed by the twinges that ate away at me for what I had done. I was supposed to be level-headed, always make the right choice for those I protected as well as myself, but something had lured me into his arms as if us being together was innate. It was inexplicable. I had tried time and time again to figure it out, but I was starting to give up on why it happened. I either needed to put the incident behind me and move on, or I needed to find Draco again and demand he explain what kind of hold he had over me to make me behave in this shameful way, but the thought of seeing him again would not be good. More than likely, it would end up very similar to our first encounter. I didn't want to put myself in that position again, but then my heart would start pounding as I thought of his strong arms wrapped around my waist, the stormy shade his eyes took, and an ache grew deep inside of me. I longed to see Draco. It was wearing on my every move and had me losing focus over the task at hand.

The couple was still at it, but now it was becoming more physical. He had pushed her backward a couple of times. She still came at him, though, her finger pointed right in his face.

The curtains moved as a slight breeze ruffled them. I looked up to see a male angel with reddish-tinted hair enter the house. His eyes were locked on me as he stood a distance away. The bickering couple didn't seem to faze him.

He seemed familiar, but it was difficult for me to hide my annoyance at his presence. I worked alone and was already distracted enough as it was with Draco continuously resurfacing in my thoughts.

"What do you want?" I snapped at him.

He didn't speak at first, which only added to my irritation. After a moment, he answered, "I'm Tabian."

I sighed. The male had grabbed hold of his wife's wrists forcefully. "I didn't ask who you were. Why are you here?"

The way he hesitated before speaking grated on my nerves.

"I'm curious about you."

I lowered my eyebrows at him. I wanted him to leave.

"I saw you before, back at that house fire a little while ago," he stated, and it dawned on me where the familiarity was coming from. He had swooped down to watch what was happening on his way through during that particular fire. He had annoyed me then also. "You don't like to be around others much, do you?"

"I'd rather be by myself. That includes right now."

The angel that called himself Tabian smirked.

"I do get the hint..." He looked up at me, a hopeful gleam in his eye.

I sighed. "I was that blunt, huh?" I asked flatly.

Tabian continued to watch me. I tried not to look at him. I was pretending to be concentrating on the human couple before me, waiting for my moment to intervene. I didn't interact much with the other angels. Conversing with others was a waste of time. I'd rather just keep busy with the duties I was supposed to do. We were constantly being sent on missions, to comfort and protect a set number of humans. We knew when difficult times were going to arise for them, and that is when we were to be there. One day you'd see an angel, and the next they'd be gone on another mission, sometimes on the other side of the Earth. It didn't make sense to make friends with an angel that was only going to be around for 2 days. What was the sense in telling someone things about yourself and then turning around and telling a different person the same thing the next day?

"Sarenah, you're a warrior angel."

"I am," I replied, being rather short with him.

"So why these mundane tasks?"

My irritation with him increased. "I'm merely following orders."

"I just find it a little strange, don't you? I mean, you're strong and able for combat."

"Who am I supposed to be combating?" I snapped.

Tabian paused for a moment before saying, "Why, evil of course."

"I'm following orders," I repeated, my tone monotone and dry. "We're not supposed to question the orders."

42

The woman cried out at her husband's arm stretching out before him as he got ready to swing at her, but he decided against it and lowered his arm as he continued to yell obscenities her way.

"I'm not trying to make you second guess yourself..."

"What are you trying to do?" I asked, now staring him straight in the eyes so I could glare at him.

He chuckled.

"Did I miss something funny you said?"

He shook his head.

"Because as I'm following orders, it seems that you are not, unless you've been ordered to be here to try my patience."

He just stared at me for a moment. "Like I said, you just interest me. I think someone with your potential could be doing something much better than...this."

Why was he trying to get under my skin and question what I was supposed to be doing? Mundane? What exactly was it that he did that was so much more exciting than what I did? I wanted to ask to rub it in his face, but at the same time, I didn't really care. I wanted to be left alone.

"You need to lighten up," he said, a smile still playing on his lips.

I clenched my fists together. "You need to go away before I use some of my warrior potential on you."

He studied me. "Such a temper you have, Sarenah."

"I am not in the mood for chit chat."

"You're grumpy."

"It's taking a lot of self-control not to lose it on you right now, *Tabian.*"

A shrill shriek came from the human female before me. Her husband had just backhanded her. She stumbled backwards, landing on the floor. *Funny, I feel like doing the same thing to this annoying angel beside me.* The human male stormed out, leaving her behind. She stayed on the floor, her hand pressed against the fresh bruise on the side of her face. I gritted my teeth together and looked over to the angel. Why was he still here?

"You're not leaving, are you?" I asked.

He crossed his arms in front of him. "Why does my being here bother you so much?"

"Fine." I let out an exasperated breath. "If you won't leave, I will." I headed for the window and got ready to launch.

"Wait! Sarenah!" he cried out.

With that, I took the plunge out of the building. As I began to fly, I heard the angel call out to me again. "You haven't completed your orders here!"

4

Tabian

Sarenah detested me. She detested me so much that she was willing to go against orders just to get away from me.

I stood there at the window, knowing she wasn't coming back, as she disappeared into the distance. I wasn't sure how this made me feel. It was as if I was some sort of diseased creature, so deformed and ugly that she couldn't even stomach the thought of looking my way.

Behind me was the human female, writhing in her own grief over her abusive husband. She was supposed to be receiving comfort from Sarenah, her angel.

Sarenah was rebellious, but then again, so was I. I had orders to watch over Sarenah, but only from a distance. I was specifically instructed not to speak to her, but somehow couldn't resist. She was intriguing, the only angel with black wings, and her beauty suppressed all others. She liked to keep to herself which was even more alluring.

I looked to the human female. She sobbed. What an insensitive action on Sarenah's behalf. I walked over to her and bent down, placing my hand on her

47

back, and closed my eyes. I could feel the torment within her relinquishing at my touch. It was just enough comfort to get her to stop crying, and she wiped her eyes with the back of her hand, her makeup smearing to the side of her cheek. I had helped clear her thoughts.

This had been Sarenah's job.

What was it about Sarenah that made her seem discontent? Our kind were peaceful, pleasant creatures who thrived on the notion of helping others. I hadn't meant to upset Sarenah when stating she should be doing something more than comforting her group of humans, that she was a warrior and should be helping out in stronger battles than these. It had me wondering if she had been ordered to do busy work to keep her away from more important matters. The curiosity within me grew. She was becoming almost like an addiction to me. Her mystery was something I craved to unlock.

There was something happening surrounding Sarenah. Angels just weren't ordered to watch over other angels. I was going to unravel it all.

I stood up and moved back to the window and stared out into the sky. I had to go find where she went. I had to figure out what was happening, even if it cost me everything.

5

Draco

Sweat dripped from my brow. I felt the tremors begin again but tried to shake the haunting thoughts from my head that this silence and darkness could go on forever.

I had no idea how long I'd been in this cage. Time meant nothing in the pits of hell. It was all one long, horrifying nightmare. When was this torture going to end?

Keep it together, I told myself. Losing it would mean defeat, and I was not one who could be defeated. I had to get control, but it seemed, as the silent humming continued, I would slip a little bit further into a darkness within my own mind, one that wasn't as easy to slither out of.

I kept coming back to the same question: *why am I in here?* What could I have possibly done? I was loyal, dragged to the depths of darkness a long time ago where I built up my strength from mission to mission, always succeeding, and never backing down from a challenge. I had made a name for myself. I was someone everyone feared, yet respected. Damn them for putting me here.

This *had* to be a test of some sort. It just wasn't making any sense. I had killed others, dragged others to their doom, beaten and been beaten time and time again only to get back up and do it all over again. I was loyal to the darkness. I was a leader, and those trained under me were privileged to have seen my face. This...was humiliating. This was the kind of thing that could break someone, because no matter how hard I tried, sometimes the mind was one's greatest enemy and downfall. I knew I wasn't immune from the demented grasps of my own mentality. Fear was everyone's demise. Everyone held fear within them of some kind. It was a weakness, something that was hard for someone like me to swallow, as I was usually the one unleashing fear on others.

The only thing saving me was thinking about *her.* It angered me now that I hadn't gotten her name. All I had was a face and a memory of her body entangled with mine for only a brief moment, and when I had looked into her eyes, she wasn't afraid of me. Of all the women I had in my arms before, fear was an absolute in them all. That's what singled this one out, and why had we been so quick to reach out and cling to one another? It was the oddest, yet most sensual, moment of my existence. As I relived that moment over and over in my head, the picture of her long, flowing hair and lips crashing into mine was my only mechanism of comfort.

I didn't know how I was going to do it, but as soon as I was released from here, if that was ever going to happen, the first thing I was going to do was hunt down this unusual female. I'd demand her name, and have her in my arms once again. Whoever she was, she was keeping me sane right now, and she didn't even know it. I longed to know if she was thinking of me, too.

Something shuffled outside the cage. Every inch of me tensed to listen. Had it been footsteps or was my head starting to pound again?

The clang of metal against metal awakened my senses. I wanted to call out, but hesitated. I couldn't sound afraid or full of desperation, and if I spoke, it may give away both of those things.

"Draco?"

At the sound of my name, I knew instantly who it was. Vex. If ever I could title someone my *friend* here in the deepest, darkest regions of evil, it was him. He always had my back, was loyal to me. My heart leapt at the relief I felt when I realized it was him.

I stood up, stretched my neck up high, and even though I knew we couldn't see each other, I thought it would help disguise my sense of forlornness.

"I'm here," I said. I was surprised how steady my voice came out, but it only gave more confidence when it did. "Where else would I be?"

I could hear Vex sneer. "No, I suppose there's no escaping this...but if one person could, it'd be you."

Again, he revived my hope of having someone to talk to. He knew how strong I was. Perhaps everyone else was wondering if I'd be the one to escape this cage, too. Perhaps they *feared* the notion. I walked over to the door of the cage, following the sound of his voice.

A match was lit and a small lantern cast its soft glow. I squinted my eyes as they adjusted and then looked at Vex, his long, bony fingers wrapped around the bars as he peered in at me.

"How long have I been in here?" I asked.

"Do you really want to know the answer to that?" he asked back.

I tilted my head to the side for a moment, considering if this information would further taint my mentality. "No," I replied.

"I've come to check on you. I've been...worried," Vex said as he pulled back on the hood covering his head to reveal his face to me. He looked aged, as if he really had been worrying about something.

"I'm fine."

"Are you?"

I, too, gripped the bars, my eyes searching for some weakness in the metal to reveal itself to me. This wasn't any ordinary metal. This was metal made to confine the most disgusting creatures in the world in the gates of Hell with nowhere to turn to escape.

"Do you know why I'm here?"

Vex looked at me in shock. "You mean...you don't know?"

I studied his face, his eyes in particular, but he was still mostly a shadow by the dull lantern's light. "No one's told me."

Even in the dark, I could see him frown.

"If you know, tell me."

"I just figured you did know."

"How would I know?!" I yelled out, my temper exploding as I attempted to shake the bars, taken aback when they actually moved slightly.

Vex took a step backward at the outburst. "Okay, okay. I'll tell you. It never crossed my mind that you didn't know."

I bit my lip, trying to hold back the urge to crash my entire body into this metal door. My heart was thumping twice as fast as normal as the adrenaline coursed through me. I needed answers now.

"Take your time, Vex," I mumbled through gritted teeth. "I have a lot of it these days."

He fumbled with the handle of the lantern. "Draco, you crossed the line."

"Crossed *what* line? I've been nothing but faithful and devoted to everything I've been instructed to do..."

"Yes, that's true, until recently..."

My mind was again racing with what it could possibly be. "I have no recollection of what occurred recently, Vex." He knew he was trying my patience.

He leaned in closer now as if someone would hear what he was about to say. "The girl," he whispered.

"The girl? What?" I let the words sink in. Then it all flashed before my eyes again, the embrace, the look in her eyes, the kiss. "The girl...she's not one of us?"

Vex snorted out a laugh. "Not even close."

My stomach felt like it turned inside out. "How can that be? She looked..."

"Dark?" he asked, finishing my thought.

I nodded, my hand lifting to my hair to shove back the oily strands from my face. I felt as if my entire being was in turmoil. What had I done? "How bad is it, Vex?"

"Bad," he replied instantly.

"Who is she?" My eyes were on him intently as I needed to know her name, practically thirsted for it in my dungeon cell, and was just waiting for it to be revealed.

"She's trouble, Draco, an angel."

An angel?

"Sarenah."

At the mention of her name, my heart plummeted along with my stomach. "No," I gasped. "It couldn't have been her."

Rumors of the notorious warrior angel had reached my ears on numerous occasions. She was the rebel angel who led those of the darkness to their demise. Her strength and honor were well known to all. Our paths had never crossed before, until that day, the day we were like two magnetic forces being pressed together as if we had known each other for an eternity.

There was one very strict rule for our kind. We were never to mingle with those of the light. They were our archenemies. And this is something that I thought would never be a problem as I detested every single one of them for their acts of goodness and for trying to destroy everything we had worked so hard to obtain. How could I have not known? The horror of it tore me to pieces inwardly. And why would she have allowed herself to be in my presence, in my arms in such an enticing manner? This just didn't make sense.

"I swear, Vex, I didn't know," I finally blurted out once my swarming thoughts began to somewhat settle.

He shrugged. "I believe you, Draco, but as I've stated, a very serious line has been crossed."

"But she was so beautiful, and she didn't look illuminated like the rest of them do..." I was now desperately searching for an excuse for my absurd behavior.

"It's Sarenah, Draco. She has black hair, black wings. She's not like the others in any way, which has seemed to make her so powerful," he explained.

I was so distraught that the one thing I had been dwelling on, the one woman's face that had kept me sane while locked inside this cage, was the reason why I was in here to begin with. "I don't know what to say."

"I really don't know if there's a way out of this mess," he told me, as if knowing I was trying to find some hope in his words. "The masters are very displeased."

I lowered my head. "Well, if that's the case..." I didn't want to finish my thought. To think that I'd be in here forever was too unbearable to consider.

"My sincere apologies, Draco," Vex whispered, speaking as if someone had been annihilated, that someone being myself.

My temper flared once again as I thought of this *Sarenah*. I no longer felt passion toward her, longing to be in her arms again, but rather longing to tear her to shreds. "This had to have been a trap!" I yelled out. "They brought her to me so that I'd be seduced, knowing I'd be thrown in here if the line was crossed!"

Vex stared silently at me for what seemed like an eternity before speaking. "You know that can't be, Draco."

"Why the hell not? It's the only rational explanation..."

"Draco," he said as if to dissuade me. "You know as well as I do that the same rule applies to them."

I grasped the bars again if only to hold myself up. As soon as the words came out of his mouth, I knew them to be true. It wasn't a trick. The same line had been crossed with her, too. Perhaps she was serving some sort of punishment for it as well. That thought didn't sit well with me. I didn't know which way to turn. I felt as if I had been betrayed by my own heart. I lowered my head.

"I have to go, Draco."

I didn't say anything as the light of the lantern was blown out. The silence and darkness had returned, and along with it my shallow breaths and the realization that I had been the cause of my own ruin.

6

Vex

As I left the dungeons, I couldn't hide the smile forming on my lips. Poor Draco. He hadn't even known why he was being punished, yet I had already known that. I could have gotten in trouble for telling him about Sarenah, but it was just too juicy and tempting not to tell him. I would've missed out on him lowering his head in failure. It was a picture I'd always truly treasure in my mind. The great Draco had finally gotten what he deserved, and now I could take his place. Sure, he thought of me as a comrade, a friend even. The word friend left a sickening taste in my mouth. He was a fool to have ever trusted me.

I'd had to stand back and watch for what seemed like forever as he won the favor of all the dark masters. He had become their favorite. *Draco is the most intelligent...Draco is the most powerful...send Draco, he never fails...*Well, now, his weakness had bared itself to everyone. He had fallen at the hands of a woman – Sarenah, the warrior angel, of all things. A snicker escaped from my throat. I glanced around to see if anyone had heard. The eyes of the shadows were on me, but I was satisfied that they were too stupid to understand the pure joy surging through me at that very moment.

I wasn't supposed to tell him why he was being locked away. They said it was of utmost importance that he remain *calm*. Did they really think that Draco could get upset enough to bring down the whole dungeon with his wrath? Ridiculous, every single one of them. He had put on a good show for a very long time, but now it was time for him to wither away to nothing in the midst of his own fears. It was *my* turn now. Nothing could have delighted me more than to be the bearer of his bad news, that his precious Sarenah was an angel. The news would surely tear him apart.

I was already making headway on becoming the new commander. It was difficult to contain my excitement. Oh, I'd be back to visit poor Draco, to watch him suffocate in his own terror and delight in it while I told him of things happening on the outside, of how well the tables had turned for me. I'd make sure to do it in a very sincere way. He did confide in me, after all.

Another snide smirk made its way on my lips. I found myself covering my face with my hand. Happiness was very much frowned upon here.

I looked up to see an advisor headed my way. A pang of nervousness came over me as I made sure to wipe the arrogance away from my face before he got too close.

"Vex, I need to have a word with you," he said, his face inches away from mine.

I nodded, hurrying after him to one of the corridors to get some privacy. I hoped he didn't know what I did. Surely he couldn't possibly know.

"It's done, Vex," the counselor hissed.

"What is?" I asked.

He looked around to see if anyone was near. The area was empty except for us.

"Everything has been put into motion again. It's been a very, *very* long time since this has happened," he explained.

I didn't have the slightest clue as to what he was talking about. I raised my eyebrows. "I don't understand..."

"There are certain forces, Vex, which even you can't comprehend. They exist, and no matter what the circumstances, even death can't stop these forces from going into motion again. It's like a cycle that keeps happening. We've tried to prevent it, even thought that this time would be different, but it's happening again. The turmoil...can't you feel it?"

I stared at him, dumbfounded. I felt nothing but utter bliss at Draco's situation. How dare this idiot try to take away my good fortune so soon?

"I just wanted to warn you before you get carried away in it," he continued. "We can try to hold it off from happening for a little while longer, but we're unsure if we can completely stop it. It's the most powerful motion of all."

"Sir," I began, feeling as though he were speaking a foreign language to me. "How will I get carried away in this motion that you speak of?"

He grunted at both my curiosity and incomprehension.

"Draco," the counselor whispered. "You spoke with him?"

"I did."

"What kind of state is he in? Have the terrors taken over him?" he questioned me.

I bit the edge of my lip, trying very carefully to say the right thing. "My lord, he didn't seem overly disturbed by the darkness, but perhaps he was keeping himself composed in my presence."

Sighing, the counselor pulled on my shoulder to bring me closer to his face, his sharp fangs hanging out over the sides of his bottom lip. "Was he...upset?"

"Of course he was upset being locked away..."

He shook his head. "Was he angry?"

I thought about how he had shaken the bars the one time, how they had moved, but felt it was best to keep that little tidbit to myself. "No."

The counselor pulled away and let out a sigh of relief.

"This motion you speak of, does it have to do with Draco?" I asked.

He came within an inch of my face again, licking his lips grotesquely before he spoke. "It has *everything* to do with Draco."

7

Sarenah

Flying around, the morning fog was just beginning to lift from the bed of the Earth. I hadn't rested much the night before. My thoughts kept returning to Draco and how torn I had become at what had happened between us. It had been so very wrong, yet I endlessly thought about being in his arms again, feeling his chest pressed against me. I felt so disobedient to the light, but at the same time so alive. Every shadow that passed by, every creature of the dark and light that came my way, I'd turn my head quickly to catch a glance, hoping that it'd be him, that he had tracked me down to find out more about me. I doubted I filled his thoughts in the same way. Creatures of the dark didn't consume themselves with obsessions over others. Then again, neither did angels...

I was surprised I hadn't gotten reprimanded for what I had done with him. I had interacted with someone from the other side, and in a very inappropriate way nonetheless, but I had heard nothing. I was trying to keep myself busy, hoping that the time wouldn't come that I'd be asked to have a private meeting. Those were never good news when it came to me.

Sun beams broke through the clouds on the horizon. They poured down upon my black wings, making them shimmer. I pulled my long hair back with one hand while surveying the city below as the humans began their morning. They always seemed in such a hurry. If only they could understand that time was precious and not to be rushed, but I doubted they ever would. It was how their lives played out.

I tried to think back to a time before I was an angel, before I fought for the side of the good. It was like I had no memory of beforehand. Maybe there was nothing before. So why now? Why did I crave something more after all this time? Did Draco touching me change me that much?

It was all too overwhelming for me to figure out, how I felt and how I was supposed to feel, how I had acted and how I should have...it left me bitter and even more withdrawn than I had originally been. I wanted to pursue Draco, but if I acted on impulse again, that was being defiant. And if I did find him, then what? *Hi, Draco, it's me. Do you remember that time we kissed?* How many other women had been at his mercy and in that very same position? Then there was that other fact where he didn't know who I was or I'm sure he wouldn't have come a mile within my reach. I had deceived him by hiding that from him.

Wallowing in my misery, I flew down lower to the ground to get a better look at human life. They weren't that interesting to watch. I wasn't the least bit jealous of how they were. Their emotions seemed to define them. Then again, I didn't realize I had such emotions within myself before Draco...

There he was again, consuming my every thought. I needed to forget about him. I *would* forget about that mistake I had made.

Swooping down, I landed on a pole just above a busy highway and sidewalk. I decided just to observe for a moment, take my mind off this growing fury that had balled itself up inside of me.

A speeding taxi was headed down the street. A middle-aged female, dressed in a gray suit and staring at her cell phone, starting walking off the sidewalk and into traffic. It all happened so fast.

71

Within moments, the taxi collided with her. She rolled onto the hood of the vehicle and then back off again onto the pavement. She wasn't moving.

I rushed down to her side. The driver of the taxi was clumsily climbing out of his car and peering down at her. He was mumbling something and reached for his phone to call an ambulance as a crowd began to gather round.

I touched the side of the woman's face. She slowly opened her eyes and looked up at me. She smiled.

I was completely taken aback. Had she seen me? It looked as though she was staring straight at me. I took a step back.

The woman sat up.

"Are you okay, ma'am? Ma'am?" someone called out to her.

She rubbed the back of her head and then reached for the shattered cell phone by her side. "I think so," she replied. She looked at me and smiled again as she mouthed the words *thank you* to me.

My heart began pumping wildly in my chest. She *had* just seen me. Incredible. I didn't think it was possible.

A few men helped her to her feet. The taxi driver was still on his phone. He touched her on the shoulder as she turned to tell him she was all right.

"I'm a little banged up, but I'm fine. It wasn't your fault. It was me...I wasn't paying attention to what I was doing. Please, tell them not to come. I don't need an ambulance. I can manage to get checked out on my own."

The woman stepped back onto the sidewalk, and although a little wobbly, she looked unharmed. The crowd began to dissipate, and she sat down on a nearby bench. Her eyes searched in my direction, and then when it seemed she had found me, she motioned for me to come sit with her.

Frowning, I took a few steps forward. I wasn't exactly sure what I was supposed to do in this situation. The thought that a human could see me was unnerving.

"Please, sit," she said, patting the bench beside her.

73

"You can see me."

She pressed her lips together in another smile and nodded. "Yes, I can."

"But...how is that possible?"

"Please, sit down. Talk to me for a bit."

Sighing, I gave in and sat. I studied her for a moment.

"You're okay?" I asked, still wondering how she had remained intact without breaking a single bone.

"I believe you jolted me back to life when you touched my head," she replied. "Are *you* okay?"

"What kind of question is that?" I lowered my eyebrows. *I shouldn't be here. This shouldn't be happening.* It didn't feel right.

She shrugged and seemed overly pleasant. "It's just a question, Sarenah."

I gasped.

"Yes, I know who you are."

"But how?" I questioned her, looking around to see if any other humans noticed me sitting there. None of them seemed to glance my way. "How is it possible? Are there others that can see me?"

She chuckled at all the questions I was spitting out. "I'm Cynda." She raised up her hand for me to shake.

I stared at her extended arm for a moment before returning the gesture.

"There are others like me, I suppose. None that I know of personally."

"You're human?" I asked.

"And you're an angel." The way she said it was as if she were laughing at my remarks. She could see the fury in my eyes. "Relax, Sarenah."

"My name again," I said. "How do you know who I am?"

"I would never forget a face, especially not like yours. You're just as beautiful as before."

"Before..." I let the word roll off my tongue.

She clasped her hands together on her lap, her eyes skimming the people on the sidewalk in front of us. "I'm surprised I've gotten the opportunity to see you again. It must mean things are in effect."

"I've never seen you before," I stated.

She smiled, her eyes wrinkling at the sides. "Sarenah, we're old friends, you and I. You're just being protected from it all. Sometimes things happen, things I can't get into right now."

What in the world was she talking about? It was like she was speaking nonsense, but she knew my name. She could see me. It was too much to fathom.

She swallowed and continued, "We're all being punished in our own little way, some of us worse than others." She looked down at her hands and began fiddling with a ring on her finger.

"I'm not following what you're trying to tell me."

She smiled politely. "I'm not trying to tell you anything, really. It's just...good to see you again, Sarenah."

I narrowed my eyes at her. "I need an explanation for what you've already said."

"I've probably said too much already," she confessed, patting the hair in the back of her head. She looked up at me and gave me an intense stare. "Sarenah, tell me, has something happened?"

"Like what?" I asked, deeply troubled by this odd human woman.

"Have you...run into anyone out of the ordinary?"

"Besides you?"

She chuckled again. "Yes, besides me."

Draco. Surely she doesn't know about him. I rubbed my face with my palms as the frustration started to grow. "Listen, if you know something…"

"I'm trying to be your friend. I *am* your friend. You can trust me."

I sighed. "How in the world do I know that? You're a human."

"Well…sort of."

I stared at her for a moment. "You're so evasive. I'm not getting anywhere sitting here talking to you."

Cynda pressed her lips together as if deep in thought. She put her hand on top of mine. Her touch felt so warm. My initial reaction was to rip my hand away, but I decided to leave it be.

"It's difficult for me to talk to you, Sarenah. I never thought I'd see you again. I'm eternally human. That's my punishment. I can't die naturally like other humans. I know this must be a lot to take in, but I'm trying to be as honest with you as I can be. I'm not sure I should even be talking to you, but our paths have crossed, and so here we are again."

"Again," I repeated. "You said we're old friends. I have no memory of you."

She nodded. "It saddens me you don't remember, but I don't really expect you to." She inhaled the cold winter air. "We have history, you and I...and others involved. It seems like it's bound to repeat itself. They tried to stop it, put an end to it, but it looks like your love it just too powerful."

"I have no love," I quickly said. "I'm not human. My emotions..."

Cynda looked at me as if burning a hole through my brain. "Your emotions are what, Sarenah? Are they coming alive? Do you feel like you're going over the edge, to the point of no return?"

My mouth dropped open. Unless mind readers were real, this woman *did* know me.

"I can see it in your eyes, Sarenah. It's that hunger that I've seen many times before. It's getting to you even now as I speak to you. It grows in your very core." Her eyes lit up as if she fed on my surprise.

"Cynda," I said quietly as I removed my hand from under hers and clasped it together with my other one. "You're being punished for something that happened in the past, right?"

She nodded.

"Something I was involved in?"

Her hesitation irritated me.

"Cynda, please."

"You don't have to figure it all out today," she finally stated. "It seems as though you're already fighting it now."

"Fighting what, exactly?"

Her blue eyes pierced right through me. "Why, yourself, of course, Sarenah. It's always been an internal struggle with you."

I lowered my eyebrows. I didn't know what to think of this conversation, of this strange woman before me who seemed to know me better than I knew myself. I had a past. Had I been human once? And why wasn't I being punished in the same way she was? Why couldn't I remember?

"You're doing it right now, Sarenah. You're over-thinking." Cynda placed her hand on my shoulder as if trying to comfort me. "It's not as hard as it seems.

Just let go of what you think is right and wrong and follow your heart."

"I don't have emotions. I'm an angel," I reminded her.

"Are you trying to convince me...or yourself?"

I leaned back against the bench as I tried to wrap my mind around what was happening. I just wanted her to tell me straight what she knew, what on Earth she was talking about. I was sure she wouldn't tell me in a direct manner if I asked.

"Okay, Sarenah, listen."

I felt myself leaning in closer to this woman, eager for her to tell me something that would trigger a memory.

"This emptiness that engulfs you...if there's someone you've crossed paths with, someone you can't seem to let go, you have to go after them."

"Draco," I whispered, not realizing before it was too late that I had let the name escape my lips.

She grinned. "I knew it!"

"What?"

"History has a tendency of repeating itself when it comes to a love so intense, so powerful that it has no boundaries."

I closed my eyes tightly for a moment before opening them with the realization that it was either fate or pure coincidence that I had been instantly drawn to Draco. Somehow I had a life before being an angel. Whether human or not, I couldn't remember. It was as if my memory had been wiped entirely, but what was the reason? What had happened to all of us, even Cynda? She was telling me bits and pieces but nothing clear cut. I had a feeling of dread in the pit of my stomach.

"I know," Cynda whispered. "It must feel terrible not knowing, but I'm telling you all you need to know. Follow the direction of your heart, Sarenah."

"Draco." Tears filled my eyes and I didn't even know why. "It all happened so fast and then we were apart..."

"If you want to make sense of it all, go to him. Find him."

I shook my head. "I can't," I mumbled. "You don't understand. He's a creature of the dark. I've already done too much as it is."

Sucking in a breath of air, Cynda exhaled slowly. "You're fighting it again."

"Fighting what?"

"What you think is good versus bad. Some things never change."

I stood up, ready to get out of here. I had had enough of this Cynda and what she thought she knew. If she wasn't going to just straight tell me, then I was out of here. I already felt bad enough about what I had done with Draco, had allowed myself to be swept up in a moment with him, let alone having some human woman tell me that I had a history with this dark creature, that there were reasons I couldn't remember. I couldn't get him out of my head, and this just made me feel a thousand times worse. This would make me think about him even more, if that was even possible.

"Sarenah, please." Cynda stood up and tried to reach out to me as I darted away. "Okay. I get it."

"Do you?" I practically yelled at her.

82

She nodded, taking a step backward and putting her arm down. "It's a lot to swallow. I'm just so glad to see a friend. I don't have any these days..." she trailed off as her face took on a somber look. "Things happen for a reason. You're trying to push everyone away, but you must go to him, Sarenah. Find Draco. He is the key."

I spread out my wings as I got ready to launch away from this city and dive back into the depths of my solitude.

"Sarenah." Cynda's voice cracked as she said my name. "You deserve to know the truth."

I let the words sink in like jagged daggers, torturing me one by one.

"Please come and see me again. Promise, Sarenah. I've missed you so very much."

I nodded, feeling that if I said another word, I may burst into tears as a rush of emotions came over me.

Seconds later, I was miles above the city, climbing higher and higher into the blanket of clouds.

8

Tabian

I was careful not to reveal my presence as I hid behind the thick tree. It had taken me nearly a week to find Sarenah again after she flew away from the window, abandoning her orders. She was not easy to track at all, and it made it that much more difficult to know that if she saw me, she'd be off again in a flash. It made me ill to know how much she despised me, but even more determined to find her.

I finally found the beautiful warrior angel on top of a flat rock positioned on a mountain. The sun was shining directly upon her. It illuminated her wings, her hair, as if she shimmered while basking in the rays. It was truly breathtaking. Sarenah was a stunning creature, one that I adored.

Someday, Sarenah, you will grow to appreciate my affection for you.

I could never tire of the feeling this angel gave me – from the moment I finally found her, an exasperating thrill of the hunt, to just observing her from a distance as she had her own serene moment atop that magnificent peak. I was ordered to watch over her, but now that I had come into contact with her, listened to her harsh words, things had stirred

85

within me. I would watch her, yes, continuously. I was utterly obsessed with Sarenah. The way she tilted her head, her hair flowing down past her waist as if she were trying to feel the warmth of the sun...my heart pounded with the mere thought of being able to share this moment with her. What I wouldn't give to know what she was thinking about this very second.

She stood up and walked over to the edge of the rock. She wiggled her bare toes to the jagged end and peered down as if thinking about jumping without spreading her wings, as if the feeling of falling could ease whatever internal pain she was suffering.

I wanted to rush over to her, to take her in my arms and comfort her, but no, she wouldn't have any part of it. I had just found her. I couldn't let her glide through my fingers so soon.

The expression she held while looking over the cliff...her jaw was clenched as if measuring something. The way she carried herself was no longer serene. No. Sarenah was jaded with her existence of being an angel. She spread out her magnificent black wings and launched.

I blinked several times before realizing that she was gone. Panic seized me as I, too, launched, my eyes searching through the dense clouds for any sign of my lovely angel.

I desperately searched, flying as fast as I could. *Oh no, I've lost her again.* My heart sank at the mere thought that I would have to wait any length of time to see her again. How could I have let her slip away so quickly?

Sweat beaded my brow as I flew as fast as I knew how. Up ahead, I caught a glimpse of a dark shadow soaring through the sky. Sarenah. My heart thumped wildly in my chest as I attempted to get closer. She flew so fast, much faster than myself, and with such ease and grace. Then all of a sudden she dropped and plummeted toward the Earth floor.

I was out of breath by the time I caught sight of her. She was standing in front of a grocery store, staring in through the glass windows. She turned her head in my direction. I darted behind a parked car along the street. Slowing rising, I looked through the vehicle's windows to where Sarenah had been. She was gone. Stomping my foot on the pavement, fury grew within me at how easy Sarenah could slip through my fingers, and gracefully at that. She was here one moment, gone the next, as if popping in and out of thin air. She made it almost impossible to track her. The curiosity I had for her intensified.

Running now, my long gown was catching on my heel. I jerked at it while rounding a corner that led to an alley, and almost ran right into Sarenah. She had her back facing me. I held my breath for a moment. She didn't know I was there or else she would've lashed out at me by now. She seemed to be fixated on something...

I looked past her to get a glimpse of the scene in the narrow corridor. There were homeless people lined up against the cold wall. Some were huddled together, some alone. Kneeling down in front of some of them were dark spirits or creatures of the dark. They were whispering in some of their ears, tempting them. I couldn't hear what they were saying, but every so often a snicker would escape their filthy mouths.

I wondered why Sarenah was here just watching as if mesmerized. We had seen the dark creatures go about their work all the time. I personally tried to ignore them, stay out of their paths as if some of their disgustingness could rub off on me if I were to get too close.

She took a few steps forward.

Was she ordered to be here to comfort one of these poor souls? It was possible, but there was something odd about the way Sarenah was positioning herself as if she weren't waiting, but rather deciding. She had an uneasiness about her that was making me feel more uncomfortable as the seconds ticked on.

Sarenah walked over to a homeless man. He seemed to be sleeping as she bent over to be closer to him. I thought she was going to place her hand on him to comfort him when I saw her reach out and instead touch the dark creature on its shoulder.

The creature jumped up in alarm, making a hissing noise as if her touch had just burned its skin. Sarenah narrowed her eyes at it.

"I need to know answers from one of your kind," she said rather loudly. "Can you help me?"

Another hissing sound escaped its mouth. It looked from Sarenah to the homeless man and back to Sarenah before scurrying away like the little worm it was without giving her an answer.

Sarenah went to the next dark creature and instead of gently touching this one, she grabbed hold of its shoulder and ripped it backward. "How about you? Can you tell me anything about Draco?"

This one, too, slithered away from her reach as quickly as possible. Sarenah stood up and headed straight to the other end of the alley. I waited until she disappeared into the dreary depths of the corridor before hurrying after her, back out into the light of day. She was already well on her way to flag down another dark creature.

My hand covered my mouth in alarm at what she could possibly be doing. We weren't allowed to have interactions with these beings. There were boundaries made for us and these were strictly not to be crossed, but here I was, witnessing Sarenah doing this forbidden act, and all I could think about was why? Was she trying to get herself thrown out of Heaven?

90

"What right do you have talking to *me?*"I heard it ask her as I got close enough to hear.

"That doesn't concern you," Sarenah snapped. "I'm looking for someone."

"Who may that someone be?" it questioned her, its face too dark to make out any facial features.

The muscles on the side of her face twitched as she clenched her jaw shut for a moment. "Draco. Can you take me to him?"

"Draco?" it hissed, the surprise in its voice evident.

The name registered in my head. He was well known as an equivalent of Sarenah, only his loyalties were to the darkness. He was reputable for being a great warrior, diligent without conscience. Many from our side had been ended by his hand. Why was Sarenah asking to be taken to him?

"What are you, exactly?" the creature questioned her.

Sarenah sighed as if having to think hard about what her answer would be. "An angel."

I didn't know what I was supposed to do here. I wanted to haul Sarenah out of here and talk sense into her, but I was almost afraid to get involved in whatever it was that she was trying to do. My own devotion could be questioned here. I felt my hands begin to tremble. I immediately clenched them together.

The creature took a step away from her. "I thought so at first, but now...how can that be? You have this darkness about you..."

I watched in horror as Sarenah released her wings from her back. She placed her hands on her hips. Even the dark creature gasped.

"You're Sarenah!" it exclaimed.

"You've heard of me?"

"You're the only angel with black wings."

A smirk crossed her lips at the fear the evil being had at the mere mention of her name. "Then you know what I can do to you."

It took another step away from her.

I couldn't stand here and watch this go on anymore. Sarenah wasn't in the right state of mind. Surely she had gone insane. No one sought out the wicked ones.

"Stop!" I cried out, waving my hands in the air and rushing to Sarenah's side.

At the sight of me, it looked as if Sarenah wanted to kill me, her glare was so piercing.

"Another angel," the dark creature mumbled before slithering away and disappearing.

Sarenah tucked her wings back in as she stared at the spot where that thing had just been standing. "What are you doing?" she practically screamed.

I attempted not to be intimated by her anger. "Me? I can ask the same of you."

She clenched her teeth together, her nostrils flaring as if on the verge of unleashing her wrath upon me. "Do you have nothing better to do than stalk me, *Tabian?*"

The way she said my name chilled me. "Someone has to. Have you gone insane? You're asking for Draco now? Are you trying to get yourself kicked out?"

"So many questions, none of which I'm required to answer, you idiot." She stormed off down the street.

I ran after her.

"Are you really that stupid? I don't want you around."

"I get that, Sarenah, but I'm trying to be your friend."

"I don't need a babysitter."

"Someone needs to knock some sense into you."

She stopped suddenly and turned to face me, her expression full of hatred and disgust. "Well, what are you waiting for, then? Try and knock some sense into me."

Did she want me to resort to physical violence? "Whatever's going on with you, I'll try to help, but this...talking to demonic creatures, uttering names like Draco, how do you foresee that ending up, Sarenah? You're wreaking trouble upon yourself."

"This," she said. "What you're trying to do...get information out of me...it's not going to happen."

"I'm not prying..."

"You are."

I ran my fingers through my hair in frustration. "Because I care about you."

She stood there open-mouthed for a moment. "What does that even mean, Tabian? You don't even know me."

"You won't let anyone know you. I've been trying..."

She shook her head. "Let me make this clear for you. Listen to me, Tabian." She motioned for me to watch her lips. "I don't trust you."

I didn't know what to say to her. She was completely impossible, and I couldn't just take off. I wanted her to confide in me.

"What have I done for you not to trust me?"

She placed a finger to her lips. "What have I done to make you *care* for me?"

I just stood there feeling as if that physical violence she had been hinting at earlier would be a million times less painful than what I was experiencing internally right now. She was just so intense and unlike any other creature of the light. I was ordered to watch her, but now innately wanted to protect her.

"Are you in danger, Sarenah?"

She waved her finger in the air, gesturing for me to be quiet. "Wait a minute." She studied my face which seemed to instantly heat up and flush. She walked a circle around me before staring me straight in the eye again. "You know I want you gone, but yet here you are still. Tabian, tell me, have you been ordered to watch me, make sure I don't slip up?"

The loud exhale that escaped from my mouth gave me away, but I felt as if I couldn't breathe. She had this invisible grip on my throat as if the words she had just said were suffocating me.

She narrowed her eyes. "What were you told?" she asked.

"Nothing," I managed to spit out.

"Surely you were told something about why I'm to be watched."

I wished I did have something to tell her. At least maybe that way I would earn a little of her trust, but the fact was they hadn't told me anything except to make note of her every move, which hadn't been the easiest task. I felt like a blubbering fool around her. I wanted to wrap my arms around her and comfort her. I know she needed it, to let out everything that had built up inside her, but if I even attempted a move like that, she'd probably kill me for sure. She was in obvious turmoil.

Before I could say anything at all, another evil being approached us, this one more man-like but with half of his face deformed as if the flesh had been melted away.

He nodded as Sarenah turned to give him her attention. "So, you're the one that's been asking about Draco?"

9

Draco

Insomnia consumed me. I would sit there in the pitch blackness and drift in and out of nightmares, wondering if I were sleeping but knowing that I was little by little losing my mentality with each second ticking by. Sleep would be too generous. It would be too much of a needed escape from the reality that was my hell now.

I looked up and gasped. Before me was the image of Acadian, his body slaughtered by my hand. He had been my greatest victory. Just like me, he had been a strong commander of the darkness, but his greediness had gotten the best of him, and I had been ordered to contain him. I could never forget the bitter smile on his face when he turned to see who had come for him. Those connected with evil tend to forget that a pair of eyes are on them all the time no matter what. Acadian had thought he was immune to ever getting caught. He wanted more and more power until that was all that consumed him. He became careless, his pride standing in his way.

"So, you think you're just going to take me?" Acadian grinned, his hand resting on the handle of his sword that was still secure in its holder at his waist.

I stood there holding my ground, unaffected by his attempts at intimidation. "Oh, I know I am."

Acadian licked his lips and then wiped the moisture off with the back of his hand. "I'm not going to the dungeons."

"It's ordered. It's as good as done now."

"No. I'd rather be annihilated." With those words, he drew his sword and slashed my way.

Our swords collided. I stumbled backward a few steps, surprised by Acadian's strength.

"You'll have to drag my body there!" he yelled out, forcing another heavy blow in my direction with his sword.

I gritted my teeth together and fought back, my anger and adrenaline soaring with each inch of ground gained on the mighty creature of darkness until I slashed the blade of my sword again and again into the lifeless body of the great Acadian. I had stood there for a while afterward, just staring down at the lifeless corpse, cursing him silently in my head for being such a fool, for bringing this all upon himself. Those above me had praised me for a job well done. No one had gotten the upper hand on Acadian until he met his match that day...me. I vowed I'd never go down the same path as him, yet here I was cast into this dungeon.

His bloodied corpse floated closer to me. I wanted to scream but knew they'd hear me, knew that's what they wanted to hear.

This couldn't be real. I couldn't even see my own hands let alone some sort of ghost. Was I now so far gone that I was hallucinating?

I pounded on the sides of my head with both palms, slapping and wishing I could crawl right through to my thoughts. I closed my eyes tight and then counted to 10 before reopening. Acadian was gone. I breathed a sigh of relief. Perhaps Acadian had known all along, and perhaps he was right. Annihilation would be better than being locked up for eternity in the dungeons trying to cope with your own fears.

I needed to redirect my thoughts. All I could focus on now was everyone that had died at my hand, who I had given no mercy to, each of their faces popping up one by one as if standing right before me.

This wasn't fair. I wasn't disloyal as Acadian had been. I had made an innocent mistake. I couldn't just sit here and let my mind wander until I became vacant from the inside out.

Rage pulsated through me. I stood and made my way to the bars near the door and began attempting to move them. Nothing happened.

"I demand to speak with someone!" I screamed out into the empty black corridor. "Send someone down here!" I kept my ranting up until I could barely yell out anymore. My voice was raspy from overuse. I gripped the bars and pressed my forehead against them. "I will tear these bars off one by one!" My hands were trembling.

The hissing of a match being lit followed by the soft glow of a lantern was enough to make me have to shield my eyes with my hand. I squinted through my fingers to make out a face.

After several seconds, my eyes adjusted. Before me stood an advisor. I could tell by the cloak he was wearing with the red symbol of a skull on the side. I recognized him also but didn't really know him. He had always been quiet around me. I remembered

102

how I had always felt uncomfortable around him in a way. He seemed more like a shadow the way he lurked about, instead of an advisor. It infuriated me that he was the one standing there.

"Why all the commotion?" he finally asked.

I took a deep breath in, my nostrils flaring as it took all control within me to refrain from exploding in a fit of anger. "I want out."

"Impossible."

I let go of the bars and clenched my fists together at my sides. "I didn't know she was an angel," I said through gritted teeth.

The advisor remained silent again for another minute. "So, Draco, it seems you now know why you're in here being punished. How long have you known?"

"If I knew how many days, how many hours I've been in here, I'd be able to give you a more accurate estimation."

The advisor snorted as if amused. "Tell me, do you know this angel's name?"

"Sarenah."

"Hmm…" He lowered the lantern so it was hanging by his side as his face was now cast in a dark shadow. "This is very interesting news."

"It was interesting news to me as well and even more interesting to learn that you have no intentions of letting me go. I made a mistake."

"A critical one at that."

"I understand, but I didn't know. She didn't look…all bright."

The advisor made a clicking sound with his tongue. "Thoughtlessness, Draco, that's what's gotten you in here. We can't be having the foolish be commanders of the darkness."

"If I didn't know any better, I'd say this has all been a trap."

"No, no trap, Draco. If anyone set a trap, it was you to fall into your own."

"Would you mind deciphering that for me?" I snapped at him.

He remained quiet again for a while, both of us just standing there in the orange glow of the flickering lantern. "Who told you about Sarenah?"

I didn't answer. I wasn't about to tell on Vex. "Please," I whispered. "Come a little bit closer so I can tell you. I don't want...anyone to hear me."

The strange creature hesitated before finally making his way over to the bars. He leaned his head toward me so I could whisper in his ear. In one swift motion, I had both arms extending out of the bars and wrapped around his neck. He was pinned against the cold steel already squirming like a little worm. I yanked him higher so that his feet weren't touching the ground anymore. He continued to struggle which only made me flex my muscles and squeeze tighter around his neck.

"How dare you think you can keep me locked away like this," I whispered to him. "I have been nothing less than the epitome of loyal to you all, and this is how I get treated. I'll just make an example out of you right here, right now. I feel the wrath within me itching to get out. I'll satisfy a little bit of that itch right now." I wrapped my hands tighter still around his puny neck, his sharp nails digging into my flesh as he tried to claw his way out of my grasp. It was no use. This dungeon hadn't weakened me, and

105

this rage inside only made me that much more powerful. I could feel the shell that he was composed of shattering under the force beneath my fingertips. He struggled for air one last time before his entire neck caved in and collapsed. I let go and watched his body shrivel to the ground, the lantern turned on its side in the position where he had dropped it.

Let them come one by one. I'll lure them close enough and destroy them all.

Footsteps echoed down the corridor. Another lantern was headed my way. A smile played on my lips. Victim number two was almost here.

"Draco?" the voice said questioningly.

I looked up to see Vex standing right behind the advisor's empty corpse. A sense of relief washed over me to see someone familiar.

"What have you done? How did this happen?"

"He wouldn't let me out, called me foolish. He got too close to me, so I took advantage." I wiped a strand of hair from my eye as I peered through the bars at someone I used to stand side by side with. How I envied his position right now.

106

To my surprise, Vex started laughing. He buckled over and held his stomach from the laughter. After he was finished, he stood upright again and stared in at me. "What don't you get about this situation?" Vex asked.

My abdomen twisted at the harsh tone he was using.

"This is what your existence has led to, Draco...darkness, caged in like the wild animal you are. You're stuck. There's no escaping this. You haven't even a glimpse of hope."

I licked my dry lips and closed my eyes just then, letting the fury work its way through me as his words continued to sting me long after they had already been spoken.

"Aw, what's the matter, Draco? Have I surprised you?" Vex chuckled, a smile fixated on his face. "Everyone has a weakness. I, for one, know how alluring women can be, but an angel...especially Sarenah..." He snorted. "What *were* you thinking? Oh, that's right. You weren't thinking at all. Mistakes, my dear friend, mistakes are what gets you locked away in a place in this corner of Hell."

"So I suppose you have it all figured out, *my dear friend.*" It took all I had to hold myself together as I spoke. "With me in here, you take over, is that right?"

Vex giggled in delight. "Oh, yes, yes. That's the plan, indeed. For what seems like an eternity I have lived in your shadow, and now...well, now it's my turn. Everything is already in progress. I've begun commanding my own team."

"What makes you think they'll listen to a little worm like you?"

He thought about it for a moment before answering, "If they don't, I'll make examples out of them by killing them off one by one."

"Until you don't have a team left?"

"If that's what it takes. New teams are easy to come by."

The sound of feet dragging along the cement floor echoed down to where we were.

"You know, you are right about something," I stated.

Vex was still laughing. He was lucky he was beyond my arm's reach.

"Mistakes do get you in here, but at least I'm still alive. I'm still breathing."

"Call it what you will, Draco. You're finished. I won't have to set eyes on you ever again."

The shuffling noise grew louder.

"You're right. You won't."

Vex's eyes darted around in the direction of the sound.

"You're the one finished here, Vex."

"What?" he stuttered, his eyes locked on the dark corridor stretching out before him.

I chuckled. "Seems like you're the one who's made a mistake." I stared at him, the sweat glistening on his brow even in the dim light. "They know, Vex."

"Know what?" he whispered.

"Know you're the one that told me...about Sarenah. Tell me, did they warn you to keep your mouth shut?" I questioned him.

He shook his head. "Impossible!" he shouted out. "They don't know. They can't see."

Now it was my turn to chuckle. "There are eyes everywhere in the pits of Hell. They're coming for you, Vex. It sounds like they're *very* displeased with your disobedience."

The shadows were quickly approaching Vex before he finally realized what I said was the truth and let out a high-pitched squeal as they attacked. There was nowhere to escape. The shadows now consumed my once-comrade. He fell over as their weight crushed him. I watched until the flames within the lanterns were snuffed out by the shadows and all that was left was Vex's tormented scream.

10

Sarenah

"Something on your mind, Marta?" I glared at the other angel. She had been circling me all morning as I completed my orders. Tabian was on a tree branch overhead, too. As much as he perched, he might as well be a bird.

She swooped down to the ground. We were in a grassy meadow, tiny daisies dotting the landscape. A crease formed on her forehead as she clamped her hands together in front of her and turned to face me.

"I'm worried," Marta finally said.

That much was apparent. "About what?"

She ran a hand over her brown wavy locks. "Sarenah, there have been whispers..." She looked up at me with her big eyes.

I glanced up at Tabian who was getting ready to fly down to us. "Don't tell me there's been gossip, Marta," I said dryly.

"Not gossip, Sarenah, just serious talk about a serious situation. Concern is more like it."

I felt a small twinge of panic knowing what she said wasn't going to be good. However, Marta always had to say her piece. It was the only way she could make *herself* feel better. There was no way of getting out of the impending lecture headed my way now. "Let's hear it." Tabian was now at my side. I could feel him staring at me. I didn't give him the satisfaction of acknowledging his presence. He was like a leech. He had been following me everywhere, and there was really no way of ditching him except flying away as fast as I could, and even then it was only a matter of time before he found my location again.

"You're going, aren't you?"

"Going where?" I snapped at her.

Marta pressed her lips together as if trying to be careful about her choice of words with me. "I don't know exactly, but it looks as if you're leaving. You're already mentally there, aren't you?"

I sighed. Marta was trying my patience. It didn't help to have Tabian here, either. The sight of both of them together ganging up on me made me almost on the verge of losing my temper. "Are you a mind reader now, Marta?"

"Why are you so impossible?" Tabian butted in. "It's not hard to tell that you've been distraught

113

recently. You're not yourself. Something *is* on your mind."

"I wish I could read minds." Marta frowned. "Maybe then I could better help you."

I smirked. "I don't need help."

"You're so tough, aren't you, Sarenah?" Tabian put his hands on his hips.

"Whatever," I mumbled. "Are you two done, now?"

Marta's eyes filled with tears. "I am genuinely concerned for you. You are a hard angel to approach. You do have this intimidation about you, which is probably the reason the others haven't come to speak with you. Don't you ever just want to talk things out?"

"What's going to happen is going to happen," I stated. "Sometimes things take their course."

"Something is weighing heavily upon you," Marta said in almost a whisper. "Upon your heart."

"Her heart is leading her in dangerous directions," Tabian said. "Straight into contact with those of the darkness."

I shot a glare at him. "Thanks for feeling the need to tell her that."

He shrugged. "What's the drive behind it all?"

I thought back to when I had intentionally sought out the evil creatures lurking in the alleys at the city. I had directly asked them about Draco. The words of the last one had been lingering in my mind. I couldn't shake them from my thoughts. *Whenever you're ready, I'll take you to him. Just call out for Lune. I'll find you.* The name Lune had played on my lips for days, daring me to call out to him, knowing that when I finally did, everything would change. Many times I had thought about doing it but somehow stopped myself. I felt as if I should be prepared but had no way of knowing how to do that. How does one prepare themselves for going into the pits of Hell?

Marta swallowed, the crease in her forehead becoming more subtle. "Between that and the witch, your rebellion is getting the best of you."

I narrowed my eyes at her. "Witch?"

Marta's eyes darted to the ground.

"Wait a minute." My mind raced. What was she talking about?

"I misspoke," she quickly corrected herself.

I stared at her, trying to figure it out. She avoided my gaze. *Cynda.* "Surely you don't mean..." I turned my back to her. "But you *do* mean it."

"What are you both talking about?" Tabian asked.

"What is your infatuation with her?" Marta's tone suddenly turned cross and was aimed at Tabian. She had slipped something huge, and there was no turning back on what I'd heard.

Tabian stood there open-mouthed. "I'm trying to help!"

I rolled my eyes. "He's a nuisance."

"There have been whispers about you, too, Tabian." Marta crossed her arms.

The male angel lowered his head. Maybe I should have Marta around more often. Seemed like she could hit Tabian where it hurt the most and get him to shut up.

"Back to what you were saying..." I reminded her.

"I wasn't saying anything." She turned as if getting ready to launch. "I can clearly see you're going to do what you intend to do. No one's going to change that mind of yours."

116

"You can't go," Tabian protested. "You haven't said your piece."

"I've said too much," Marta replied.

"An eternal witch," I mumbled. "She's neither in Heaven or Hell. She's bound to wandering the Earth..."

"Who is this witch?" Tabian asked. "Witches are evil."

"No," I said softly, my brain working on overload trying to fit all these pieces together. Cynda could see me. She had spoken as if we had known each other for...forever. "Not this witch."

My words had kept Marta there for another moment.

"I'm right, aren't I? She's good."

"Who?" Tabian repeated.

We both ignored him, turning our attention to a shadow overhead. The wind rustled my hair as he landed, his huge, muscular frame turned to me, his gray eyes piercing into me.

"She's both good and bad," Saint stated as he dusted off a spot on his wing.

At his words, Marta launched into the sky.

117

Saint shrugged. "Well, that's a first."

"What is?" I asked.

"Marta not sticking around to hear what everyone says." He chuckled.

I smirked. Saint wrapped his large arms around me and gave me a hug. I welcomed the comfort of his affection and leaned in against his chest, just needing a moment to not think about anything and just be. After several minutes like this, I looked up at Saint's face. His jaw was clenched. I pulled away to see what was bothering him. He was glaring at Tabian and Tabian at him.

"Why is this guy here?" Saint asked.

"I should ask the same of you," Tabian huffed.

"He's my stalker," I whispered.

"I heard that." Tabian crossed his arms to pout.

Saint eyed him up and down. "Need me to get rid of him?"

I shrugged. "Good luck. If you do, he'll only be back."

Tabian grinned.

"She doesn't like you, pal." Saint clenched his fists at his sides, his muscles bulging as he did so.

118

"He already knows." I walked away from Saint and sat down in the grass, my fingers gliding across the tiny green blades.

Saint had always been my refuge. Though not always around, he did seem to manage to find me when I needed him the most. He was my best friend, my only friend. I trusted him completely. He was strong and loyal, never judgmental. Perhaps that's what he saw in me, too. We were very much alike, and we clung together in our weakest moments. I was surprised he had come to me, yet relieved. I wasn't sure if he was on my side yet or not, but at least he was there.

"How have you been?" he whispered, sitting down beside me, his chin settling on my shoulder.

"Something's going on. Something's wrong." I plucked a daisy, root and all, and began twirling it in my fingers.

"So I've heard. There are definitely rumors."

"I don't even want to know." I examined the flower.

He raised his eyebrows. "I know you don't, but it's not just the other angels, Sarenah. You can hear your name being mumbled by the lowly creatures, too."

Not what I wanted to hear, but why wouldn't everyone be talking? I had been asking for Draco. A picture of his face entered my mind, his lips on my ear as he held me in his arms.

"So what is going on?" he asked. "Why in the world are you looking for Draco?"

"Your archenemy," I said, the words making me melancholy the moment they slipped from my lips. Draco and Saint had been at odds with each other for a very long time. I could only imagine how much I had hurt him to hear those *rumors.*

He nudged me with his chin. "What happened?"

I attempted to hold back the tears that were threatening to fall. My chest heaved as a sob escaped my throat.

"That bad?"

"How do you know about Cynda, and how do you know she's good and bad?" I managed to ask.

Saint sighed as he rose to his feet. He glanced at Tabian, who stood from a distance watching us.

I stood up and faced him. Was he hiding information from me? The entire universe could be against me, but not Saint. I had to make him understand, but how could I do that when I didn't even know myself? I could just feel this dread hovering around me like a dark cloud. The dread had been haunting me ever since I left Draco's arms that day.

"Sarenah," Saint began. "Did you ever just see someone and feel as if you just know who they are?"

A chill cut through me. I wanted to scream yes, yes, I did. I had felt that way with Draco, but I felt frozen, petrified by his bizarre words. I nodded as he went on.

"I crossed paths with the witch one time, and I had this feeling as if I knew her even though I had never seen her before. I've been fascinated by the feeling, and I go to see her sometimes."

"Have you spoken with her?" I asked.

He shook his head. "I've kept my distance."

"She can see me," I told him.

He studied my face. "So I've heard."

"Oh, yes." I pressed my lips together. "The whispers..."

"And Draco?" he asked, his eyes burning with an uncertain intensity as he waited patiently for me to answer.

I licked my lips, wanting to just return to that hug that Saint had initially given to me and try to escape from whatever reality it was that I was facing. "I don't know what happened. It's almost like what happened with you and Cynda. Only...I was drawn to him. I needed to be near him." I glanced at Tabian out of the corner of my eye as I lowered my voice. "I *desired* him."

There was no denying the grief flashing in Saint's eyes at what I had just revealed to him. "Did you touch him?" Saint asked through gritted teeth, his anger evident on his face.

I lowered my head, not wanting to see his expression.

"Sarenah, how could you?"

"You don't understand," I quickly said, defending myself. "It just happened. I...I don't know why, but it feels like..."

He took a step closer to me, his hands gliding across my shoulders and down my arms. "Like what, Sarenah?"

I let my shoulders slump in defeat. "It feels like I'm in love with him."

Saint released his grasp on my shoulders and began pacing back and forth in the middle of the meadow.

"Something's happening or has happened. I don't know, Saint. I just feel like things are being hidden and somehow I've stumbled upon something, upon Draco. They've been keeping us apart."

"Who has been keeping you apart?" Saint yelled out.

Tabian rushed to my side at Saint's outburst.

"That's just it," I told him. "I don't know. I don't know anything. It's eating away at me. I have to find out what's going on."

"Is he bothering you?" Tabian asked, his arm going around my shoulders.

I backed away from his touch.

"I don't like this guy." Saint glared at him.

"The feeling's mutual," Tabian said, standing his ground.

I pushed Tabian in his chest. "Do you even comprehend what's going on here?" I yelled at him, giving him another shove. "Are you willing to give up your eternity to follow me to where I'm going?" I could see the fear stirring in his eyes. "You're not a warrior, Tabian. You have no idea how ruthless the dark side can really be. You've seen bits and pieces, how they lure humans in and upset them. You swoop in and comfort them, but they're even more horrible than all that. They twist and eat away at your mind. They torture others in ways unimaginable. It can be much worse than just physical pain. When they get their hands on you, you'll be longing with an ache that probably will never go away...never. Are you really ready for that, Tabian? Will you ever be ready for that?"

Saint chuckled from behind me. "You're scaring the boy."

Tabian's eyes moved from me to Saint. He began trembling all over, his face turning red. "I'll show you who's a boy!" He leapt toward Saint, trying to tackle him. Saint daintily moved out of the way. Tabian ended up on his face in the grass. He just laid there for a few moments.

"This isn't a game, Tabian," I continued. "This is bad stuff. I can't even put into words what could happen."

Moaning, Tabian managed to get back to his feet and steady himself. He was visibly embarrassed. He stood no chance against Saint.

"You're really going?" he asked. "You're going to find Draco?"

"It's my only chance at answers."

"You really need those answers? You're willing to go through everything you just spit out at me yourself?" Tabian brushed his hand against the grass stain on his shirt.

I bit my lip. "Yes, I am. I can't seem to let it go."

"What's *he* to you?" Tabian asked, gesturing toward Saint.

I turned and looked at the strong warrior angel, wondering if he was going to come with me. I would be stronger with him by my side, but in the same instance I would understand if he made the choice not to. "He's my best friend." I thought I saw a glimmer of sadness in Saint's eyes. Did he feel obliged because of the title I had just given him?

"What's *she* to *you?*" Saint reiterated.

Tabian walked over to me. He brushed his fingers against mine. I instinctively jerked my hand away. He frowned and looked to the ground before staring into my eyes again. "Sarenah, I'm begging you to reconsider. Angels do not belong messing around in the darkness. We are full of light and goodness. We are supposed to be happy creatures. I don't know why you're going after Draco, but please just put it all behind you."

I stared back at him for a moment. "But you see, Tabian, I don't think I can be happy ever again if I don't find Draco."

Tabian's face twisted as if I was utterly insane. He thought I was going after Draco as if wanting to destroy him. Wouldn't the truth surprise him when it finally became known to him?

"Sarenah," he began slowly. He looked as if he were going to try to reach for my hand again but stopped himself this time. "I need you to know how I feel about you..."

"Oh, she knows," Saint butted in. "Everyone knows. I know and I've been here for ten minutes."

Clenching his fists and teeth again, Tabian glared at Saint, who merely chuckled.

"Would you like to try to come after me again?" Saint mocked him. "Teach me a lesson? Keep me away from Sarenah?"

"Saint, enough," I said sternly. I knew Tabian was a pain more so than anyone else, but I wasn't in the mood for these two to act like Neanderthals. "Tabian, if you've never listened to a single word I've said to you, listen to me now." I waited to make sure he was looking directly at me. When I was satisfied he was paying attention, I told him, "Get the idea of anything ever happening between you and me out of your head. It's not going to happen. Not ever." I wasn't sure if it registered, but I could only hope. "Are you coming with me, Saint?"

The muscular creature stretched out his large wings and drew them back in. He was absolutely stunning. I don't know why I didn't feel for him the way I felt for Draco. I had known Saint a long time and Draco barely an instant, but all I could think about was running my fingers through Draco's long black hair.

"There's no way I'm letting you go by yourself. Someone needs to protect you." Saint smiled, his entire face lighting up brilliantly.

Tabian again seemed disappointed by the fact that he was not my protector. I raised my eyebrows at him. "Well?" I questioned him. "Don't you have someone to go report to? Aren't you going to go tell them that I've decided to go find Draco?"

His eyes moved from me to Saint. "I'm coming, too."

Saint looked impressed by that decision. "Well, that's going to make this even more interesting with him tagging along. He's the kind of guy that will stab you while you sleep."

We turned around and began walking through the meadow, Saint and I hand in hand with Tabian trailing along behind.

After a few feet, Saint squeezed my hand and turned to me. "Well, let's get this over with." He stared into my eyes. "Love me?"

I smiled, thankful for the company. "You know I do." With that, I opened up my lips and said aloud the name that I had been so desperately wanting to all along. "Lune, come to me."

11

Tabian

The dark creature seemed to slither its way up through the ground and stand up in the tall grasses of the meadow. It was particularly odd to the eyes as this foggy black figure meddled its way in the middle of a gorgeous colorful scene. I swallowed hard. This was it. There was no going back on my decision now. My insides churned at the thought of what I'd done. Did Sarenah view me as a hero for my choice of not going back and ratting her out? I hoped so. Then again, my reasons for not telling on her were partially selfish as I knew that I may be reprimanded if I went back. Surely it was known now that I had disobeyed orders and interacted with Sarenah after strictly being told not to. Marta had said herself that there had been whispers about me. A wave of paranoia swept over me.

I stood in the distance while Sarenah was holding hands with that angel they call Saint as they spoke to that *thing.* I was on the verge of freaking out. I didn't want to be tormented in "ways unimaginable", as Sarenah had put it, but I couldn't stand the thought of not being with her. I was head over heels in love with her. *She may claim she doesn't want anything to*

131

do with me now, but she just doesn't know yet that I will always be on her side, that I will always be there for her. I supposed I needed to give her a little more time to make that realization. I wouldn't let her down, and the first time Saint made a wrong move or wasn't there for her, then I'd swoop in with my charismatic charm and hold her against my chest. She'd tell me she loved me, and then we could decide what to do from there. Angels weren't to be in love with one another or maintain any sort of physical relationship. That was grounds for being kicked out or some other gruesome punishment I didn't want to think about right now.

I just had to let Sarenah get whatever this was with Draco out of her system. Draco must have really struck a nerve with Sarenah for her to be this determined to find him.

I was really annoyed with how Saint was touching her. Best friends? Did best friends hold hands like that? It made me want to puke. *It should be me up there beside her.* Then again, I didn't want to be face-to-face with that *thing*. It looked putrid enough as it was from a distance.

132

"How can I trust that you're taking me to Draco?" I heard Sarenah ask the dark shadow.

Its head was completely covered by a black hood. "You can't."

Nothing about this felt right. Then again, why should it? This felt like a trap. Perhaps they were trying to turn my beautiful Sarenah into one of their own. Well, if it was a trap, I'd be there to save her.

"You coming?" Sarenah asked as she turned to look at me.

I loved the way her long, dark hair was blowing in the breeze. She wasn't afraid of that shadow. I both envied and respected her bravery.

Nodding, I stepped up beside her. The shadow dug his finger into the dirt beneath him, drawing a circle. A black hole appeared in the ground.

"Better jump in quickly before it disappears," the creature remarked before jumping in first. It seemed to suck him in.

There was no door, no easy entry, which basically meant no way out. This was the gate to Hell. Vomit made its way into my throat. Within seconds, Sarenah and Saint were throwing themselves into that hole. I closed my eyes and followed.

Moaning was the first thing I heard when I reopened my eyes. I couldn't see anyone being tortured, but there was definitely pain and suffering all around. Fear took its grip on me.

I tried to focus on Sarenah's face, tried to tell myself she was worth this extremely poor choice I had made to come along with her, but I knew deep down that this would only end in disaster. I doubted I would ever see the sunshine again. My knees buckled slightly underneath me.

"Who are you?" Someone approached us, his face mauled and blood openly seeping from his sores.

"I'm looking for Draco," Sarenah boldly said. "Take me to him."

His disfigured face twisted in disgust. "Oh, it's *you.*" He turned to look at the shadow who had brought us. "I thought she was to be alone."

The shadow hesitated. "The other two insisted on coming. I figured more to play with." It snickered.

Sarenah's body tensed. That creature had led us here with no intentions of letting her anywhere near Draco. Her uneasiness only made me quiver more.

"You were instructed to bring only her." More blood seeped from the edges of his wounds, some of them beginning to crust over now. He didn't give the shadow time for an explanation. He took out a sword and sliced the shadow in half from his head to his toes. It shrieked and disappeared into the ground beneath it. "Seize them!"

Creatures that seemed to come right out of the walls headed straight for us. Sarenah and Saint had their swords out and posed for a fight. The creatures were slow but heavy. They jumped on our backs and knocked us down to the floor. Sarenah and Saint were forced to their knees. Their hands were bound behind them. Likewise, something was being wrapped around my wrists, the material cutting into my skin as I winced from the pain.

"Take their swords," the dark creature commanded. Flickers of sparks flew up as the swords were being drug against the cold rock beneath us. "Lock them up."

135

My heart plummeted. It *had* been a trap. What a disgrace the bunch of us were as angels.

The creatures were all over me. They lifted me up and tossed me into some sort of cell. My head hit the back of the hard wall. It instantly throbbed.

I attempted to push myself into a more upright position. My fingers skimmed the floor. There was a layer of something sticky and foul covering it, getting underneath my fingernails. The stench of decomposing flesh filled my nostrils as my stomach churned once again.

Where was Sarenah? I could hear cries of pain everywhere like some sort of sick choir echoing. I couldn't imagine that one of them would be her. She wasn't the kind to likely shriek. Anger burned within me when I thought that they could possibly be beating her.

I tried to move around again, my fingertips dangling in the stickiness beneath me as they were pinned securely behind my back. My muscles were already starting to ache from this position.

I wasn't sure how many minutes went by, but finally the door opened. A lantern cast a soft glow to where I was. I could make out Sarenah's and Saint's forms being forced into the cell. They were fighting and struggling, both of them, kicking and even using their heads as weapons.

What's the use of giving up all that energy? We're outnumbered. We're angels in the pits of Hell.

I scoffed at what it was they were trying to prove with their tough-guy act. We were in *their* domain now. They would do with us as they pleased.

Sarenah wiped her chin across her shoulder. It looked like blood smeared onto her skin. Her anger sometimes led to foolish actions.

"Sarenah," I called out. "Are you okay? What did they do to you?"

She spit what I could only assume was more blood out onto the ground beside her. "You shouldn't have come, Tabian."

I frowned. No, I shouldn't have. *I shouldn't be here and neither should she.*

"How could you have trusted them?" I asked. "You should've known better."

"It's not over yet," Saint said. By the tone of his voice, he too, was in pain as he sucked in a heavy gulp of air.

"What do you mean it's not over?" I questioned him. "Look where we're at. This is where we'll die."

Saint let out a huff. "Maybe where *you'll* die, but not me."

"What exactly do you have planned, Saint?" This was crazy talk. He still thought he was stronger than everyone here.

"As soon as an opportunity presents itself to me, we're getting out of here," he explained, as if it were so simple to do.

I leaned my head back against the wall, the sore spot returning as I did so. I was the only one with any sense in this mess they had gotten us into.

"Maybe I can talk my way out," I suggested, lowering my voice in case anyone was nearby. "The next grotesque thing that presents itself, let me be the one to talk."

A noise escaped Saint's throat very similar to a snort. "Why did we have to bring him along?"

Sarenah said nothing.

"It's worth a shot!" I hissed.

"You really think you can talk your way out of Hell?" Saint shifted his position, his discomfort evident from his hands being bound, too. "I bet no soul ever in the history of being sent to Hell has ever tried to talk their way out."

His amusement fueled my anger. I was not a moron as he so indicated. "We are not souls sent here for damnation."

"No, we're angels who have willingly stepped foot into this place of desolation to protect Sarenah." He paused for a moment. "Well, I plan on protecting her at least... not sure about you."

I sucked my bottom lip in and bit down on it. How could Sarenah possibly stand to be near him? He wore his smugness on his sleeve everywhere he went. It was that kind of attitude that got you killed. Being in an alliance with him was going to get us *all* killed.

12

Sarenah

My mind was swirling. I felt agitated and exhilarated at the same time. All of my senses were on high alert. I was in Hell, the epitome of evil and darkness. I knew the odds were against us, that we may never get out of here, but the knowledge that we were somehow close to Draco made the adrenaline course through me at an alarming speed. This cell was just a place to bide our time. Saint was right. An opportunity would present itself, and when it did, we would take full advantage.

I glanced over at Tabian. He was barely visible, but I could tell he was sulking. He was such an annoying creature, one I'd like to throttle. His creepy stalking of me had landed him straight to Hell. I didn't know if Saint could put up with him as long as I had. Then again, I hadn't been in such small quarters with him before. Maybe the shadows and demons were the least of his worries. Perhaps Saint and I would murder him first. A smile crossed my lips. Maybe Tabian would be of some use to us. He could be bait. We could throw him out to the others to divert attention from us while we got away.

"You know, Tabian," I said, as I dug my heel into the floor. "It's a funny thing you bring up."

"What's that?" he asked from the other end of the cell.

"Us dying here."

"Yeah, it's such a funny thing to think about, Sarenah," he said coldly.

The shrieks of those tormented grew louder for a brief moment. "I didn't mean it like that." I sighed. "It's just interesting, don't you think, to think of death coming to creatures like us, creatures that are supposed to be immortal?"

"Well, you just saw a supposed immortal shadow being sliced in half and disappearing."

Saint was still trying to get out of his restraints.

"So that's it, then?" I asked. "When the immortal are *killed,* they just wither away to nothing?"

"You're thinking about this *now?*" Tabian questioned me.

"You're a little edgy over there," Saint remarked. "You claustrophobic or something?" He chuckled.

"I don't see how the two of you can be so relaxed at a moment like this. We have to brainstorm on how to get out."

"There's nothing to brainstorm about," Saint told him. "I told you when the moment comes, we'll think then, and think fast. We don't know what's going to happen, who it is that is going to come, so why fret?"

"Why fret?" Tabian asked, his voice low and hushed but on the verge of panic. "Look around at where we are!"

"All we have is time right now while we wait," Saint continued, completely ignoring Tabian's anxiety. "Sarenah brings up a valid point."

I let it all sink in for a moment before continuing. Were we once humans who had died on Earth and transformed into angels while in Heaven? When I thought about the past, centuries had gone by of being a warrior angel, fending off evil and helping good prevail. Those years mixed into moments here and there. It was all so routine, all done obediently and without question. Why was this something I hadn't really given much thought to before? Why now?

"Do you find it odd?" I asked aloud. "You know, that we can't remember a beginning, per se?"

"A beginning?" Tabian repeated.

I nodded. "It's like we were created out of thin air and just knew what we had to do. I have no memory of entering Heaven and becoming an angel. I don't think I've been around since the beginning of time as I have no memory of that either. Were we once humans? Have we already died physically and can now die by simply dissipating?"

"Wow," I heard Saint mumble under his breath. "You're right. I can't remember coming into existence either."

Everyone remained silent for a while as we all contemplated it.

"What about you over there?" Saint asked Tabian. "Do you remember anything?"

"No, but I think that's how it's supposed to be," he stated. "No one but God knows everything. Maybe we were once humans who died and went to Heaven and became angels. Maybe we have always been angels. I don't know. I don't think it's worth my time dwelling on it, though."

"I'm not dwelling." Geez, Tabian was so uptight.

"She's just making conversation," Saint stated.

"Yeah, just making conversation." But the thoughts of not knowing gave me an uneasy feeling. It just added to the *something's not right* feeling that had been consuming me for weeks now.

The feeling was quickly erased as Draco popped into my thoughts next, his voice deep and smooth, one of authority. *Whatever you are, you're beautiful, and I'm drawn to you in a way I can't even explain,* Draco had whispered in my ear. He haunted me, and I was thriving on that fact.

13

Saint

The glow of the lamp outside the cell illuminated Sarenah just enough that I could see her gaze shift to somewhere else. Where exactly was she now in that pretty little head of hers? She stared at the wall, her eyes suddenly glistening with a light coming from within. She was thinking about him again...Draco. The very utterance of his name, even in my thoughts, made me burn in fury. Century upon century I had fought him. He was powerful, but so was I. It was as if he were my equal, only his obedience was to the other side, the dark side. There were rumors of countless crimes and terrible, merciless acts he had committed. He was a hero in his own world for it, his world here, in Hell. I gritted my teeth together. If only I had had a chance to kill him, he wouldn't be presenting himself as a problem to me now, but somehow we had diverted each other battle after battle and neither one of us had gotten the upper hand.

Draco.

I stuck out my tongue in disgust as if on the verge of vomiting. What had he done to Sarenah to entrance her so? What kind of brainwashing games was he playing?

Sarenah had always been one to bend the rules. For this reason, we had become so close. She was reputable in being daring, which is why being a warrior angel suited her so well. It put her at the forefront of danger, something that was almost an essential for a creature like Sarenah. Then the dangerous orders quit coming. She was now sent to comfort humans and do simple tasks, things that didn't put her face to face with battles and the kind of energy that she needed to fulfill that side of her that craved it so. I was not aware of why she was no longer called upon for battles, but it was obvious that she needed more than the ordinary. And then *he* had crossed paths with her. She no longer just bent the rules, she completely annihilated the rules. The rumors spread like fire through the angel community. She was a threat to her own existence. Surely, God would kick her out of Heaven for her disobedience...at least that's what everyone had suggested.

I knew I had to find her and quickly, see what all this buzz was about. I never had anticipated it to be this bad. The never-faltering Sarenah looked lovesick. One of the most powerful and menacing forces of Hell, Draco, had lured her in somehow and captivated her.

I clenched my hands into fists behind me, the restraints digging into my skin. I felt a surge of pain go up my arm, but I didn't flinch. I had drug myself into this situation, and now I had to deal with the consequences. There was no way I was going to let Sarenah go in here all alone. When it came down to it, she was all I really had. She was forward and blunt with me, always had been, and I could count on her for anything. Looking over at her now, knowing that Draco flittered behind her eyes, my jealousy soared. Sarenah had always fascinated me. She was so strong, so independent.

My mind fluttered back to the first time I had met her. I was on my way back from battle, flying over some of the highest mountains created on Earth, when I saw her. She was standing on a cliff, her toes right at the edge, her black wings spread out around her as her coal black hair fluttered down to her ankles in the breeze. My heart had felt like it stopped for a moment. I was intrigued. I had to fly down and see this creature.

I thought I was sneaking up behind her when she spoke. "Don't think I don't know you're there," she had said.

"What are you doing?" I asked.

She motioned with her hand to stand next to her at the edge of the cliff. She stared out over the raging waters of the river below. "Look down," she had instructed me. "We always fly over things like this, but do you ever take the time to stop and just observe the beauty of nature? It's breathtaking, don't you think?"

I looked down at what she was seeing. In the distance, the river curved and met on the horizon with a setting sun, its orange hue illuminating the sky behind it.

"No," I mumbled.

"No?" she asked, turning to look at me then, her eyes scanning from my head to my toes.

I smiled then. "No, I don't usually take the time to stop and just take it all in."

She smiled back and it reached her eyes and almost made them sparkle. "Well, you really should, you know. There's beauty all around us. I'm Sarenah, by the way."

I had had a difficult time looking away from her eyes at that moment. "Saint."

Sarenah was extraordinary. I would never forget that moment and how we had sat there on that peak until the sun came up the next day and just talked, enjoying each other's company and learning all about each other. The topic had turned to her wings.

"Oh, yeah, my wings," she had said. "Always the highlight of the conversation, I assure you." She had smirked. "You really want to know why they're black?"

I had nodded, anxious for her to tell me. Never before had I encountered an angel with wings any color other than white.

"I wanted to be different, so I painted them."

I raised my eyebrows. "Really? What?"

The corner of her mouth lifted at her own amusement at what she was saying. "You know, like a Goth angel. Maybe next I'll get them pierced."

My eyes had grown large as she had exploded into fits of laughter and hit me on the shoulder with her fist.

"You thought I was serious?" she asked, holding her belly now, still bellowing out in fits of laughter.

I had felt my cheeks blush as I began chuckling along with her. "I don't know what to believe with you!"

She threw her head back, her hair falling down her back in between those magnificent wings. "Oh my, Saint, you are too funny. I'll tell you the absolute truth." She got very serious then and narrowed her eyes. "I have no idea why they're black. None whatsoever."

Sitting here now in this cell meant for nothing other than the torments of Hell, I felt my stomach ball up and tighten. The highlights of the end of this battle were to come back and find Sarenah, talk with her, sit there and just be with her. I knew Tabian could be right, this could be the end of our existence as we knew it, but at least I was sitting next to her. I had always missed her when away from her, always anxious to return and see her face, that smile of hers.

"Sarenah," I whispered, her name rolling off of my tongue without a second thought of what I was doing.

"Yeah?"

"Have you thought this through?"

Her body shifted slightly. I could tell the question irritated her.

"It's a little late to think things through now," Tabian snapped.

I pointed my finger at him. "So help me..."

"You don't scare me, Saint."

"If he doesn't learn to shut his mouth, I'm going to snap him like a twig, Sarenah," I stated loudly, my voice echoing off the cell walls.

Sarenah sighed. "I told you, it's been eating at me ever since..."

"That *moment,*" I finished for her. Jealousy swarmed over me again. I scooted closer to her, our legs barely touching as we sat side by side, our backs leaned against the wall. She didn't say anything. "He's dark, Sarenah."

"I know," she mumbled.

153

I strained my eyes to see her, my night vision unable to be accessed in these depths. "No," I said sternly. "I mean *dark*. His violence is renowned. He's a murderer. He has gone through the ranks and been promoted again and again by Satan himself because of how good he is at being bad." I thought possibly those words would get through to her. "I know, we're here already, but we can escape and get out of here. There's no use in going further if you're having second thoughts..."

"The only one having second thoughts is you."

Her words stung. She was right. I had come along willingly but more so for her protection than to go along with the absurd idea that she had a passionate moment with this hideous creature, the epitome of evil and my ultimate enemy. If I got close enough to him, I didn't know if I could refrain from strangling him, trying to rid his very existence altogether. I had to talk her out of this, get through to her somehow, someway. I couldn't just let her go to the pits of Hell alone with this idiot beside us not knowing if she'd ever return. The not knowing would kill me. There was no other answer but to say yes and to follow her. The thought of Draco touching her made me clench my fists together into tight balls. It was me she leaned against when no one else was there for her. I was the one she shared all her thoughts with. It was me and Sarenah, the warrior angels who destroyed those who defied Heaven. We were protectors and somehow ended up protecting each other along the way. She was my best friend, but more...I struggled once again with the restraints. If only angelic powers could be used, these things would've long been off my wrists. It angered me to know I couldn't reach out and touch Sarenah like normal, wrap my arm around her shoulder and comfort her.

"Sarenah," I whispered.

She looked over at me, the dim light casting shadows across her eyes that indicated weariness.

"I just want you to know that I'm here for you always." The words slipped out and made me blush in the dark room. "It's always kind of been me and you. I don't want to see you get hurt." It sounded strange coming from my mouth, but it needed to be said. She needed to know. There was so much more I wanted to say, profess my undying love to her right here and now. Even though it was forbidden, there was no denying to myself it was there. I wasn't allowed to kiss her, but the fact that Draco had…it made the fury intensify.

She bumped her knee into mine playfully. "Saint, I know." She smiled. "I appreciate it, but this is something I have to do. I know it's hard to understand, even hard for myself to understand, but I'm being drawn almost."

"He got in your head," I stated.

She shrugged. "Not in the way you think."

I wasn't getting through to her. Draco had done something to her. I was certain of it. If this is what it took to release her from his grasp, then so be it. I sat up a little straighter.

"I'm on your side, Sarenah. I'm always on your side."

14

Sarenah

I'm on your side, too, Saint, is what I wanted to say but didn't. I tried to hide the confliction that was stirring within. I had never been certain how Saint felt, but we were close, as close as two angels were allowed to be without going beyond our boundaries. We had this unspoken connection. It allowed me to be who I was when around him. He wasn't judgmental, never condescending. He didn't lecture me on how I should be acting. He had followed me straight into Hell. That gesture alone was enough to make my insides twist. He thought now was the time we should talk about it. I knew it was because of circumstance, where we were, that we may never make it back out. No matter how much he tried to convince Tabian otherwise, there was always that possibility that this is where we'd end our existence, as we knew it, as angels. But it wasn't the right time at all, not when I had Draco's face lingering at every corner of my mind.

I felt strong when with Saint. He lifted me up, encouraged me to be who I was. He loved the fact that I was different from the other angels right down to my black wings. I cherished the time we could spend together in between orders that we had to follow. We passed time together, we made memories and made it count. Battles would develop, and we'd be separated again. I thought about him often when he was away from me. Maybe I was in love with Saint. I wasn't sure what being in love meant exactly, especially with being an angel, having limitations on how I could test out an emotion such as that.

And Draco...Draco made me feel weak, drowning in an emotion so powerful, I didn't know what to do with it. I had tried to cast it away from my mind, but my heart almost ached to be near the strange, beautiful creature again. So now, I succumbed to whatever emotion this was. I cringed when the thought of it being lust entered my mind. But wow, he had been so breathtaking up close. I shuddered.

No, I refused to have this conversation with Saint here. This wouldn't be the end of us. We'd get through this, get out, and one way or another figure out what *us* meant. I couldn't allow myself to get all mushy in Hell or let my guard down in any way.

I felt slightly uncomfortable being so close to Saint knowing now how he felt, knowing that there was meaning behind his words. Suddenly Tabian cried out from across the cell.

"What's going on?" I sat up, my eyes trying to scan my surroundings. My pulse increased.

And then I felt it.

Something was crawling, inching its way up my leg. It moved faster up to my hip before slowing down again. I forced myself to become very still. It seemed as large as my palm and spider-like.

Tabian shrieked. "Get it off! Get it off!"

I desperately wanted to grab hold of it and throw it, but I hesitated. I knew where we were and that my first instincts could mean a bad decision. It made its way up near my neck just as another one hopped onto my ankle.

"What are these things?" Saint used his foot to kick one. The thing went flying to the floor only to pounce straight up and land right back on him. He huffed in frustration.

Tabian slashed around frantically as they multiplied on his body.

The one on my neck moved right behind my ear. I felt paralyzed, unsure what was happening, but I knew it wouldn't be good. Then I felt a small prick on the side of my head. It stung, but I could manage, and it didn't make me jeopardize my statue position. Then I felt the thing lift half its body in the air and slam down against my skin, sinking its teeth into me as it landed. Pain radiated like a slow burn, wrapping itself around the back of my head.

That was it. I couldn't stay still anymore. I hopped to my feet yelling, "It bit me! It bit me!" A small trail of blood dripped down the side of my head, landing on my collarbone as it still latched on like a leech. It was sucking my blood!

I thrashed around in panic as I managed to shake off the one that had been on my leg. The second it got off me, three more jumped back on in its place.

I attempted to bash my head against the wall where that thing was still attached. The creature and pain were still there. Another one bit right below my knee. Saint was now yelping out as they were attacking him. Tabian was hopping around on one foot just past him. We had no way to defend ourselves against these spider-like creatures of Hell. Fear was something I was unfamiliar with. It didn't usually surface, but I could feel twinges of anxiety rising in my chest.

More jumped on me. I was still on my feet, but they were swarming me now. It turned from ten to fifty in a matter of seconds. I couldn't see. They were covering my face, their legs in my ears. I could feel them moving. The grotesque feeling combined with the anxiousness was making my stomach churn. I was trapped, helpless, and these disgusting half-insect, half-demon things were buzzing now. One of their legs pressed through my lips and into my mouth. I spat and shook my head frantically, trying to get it out.

Sarenah.

Had someone just called for me? The buzzing was all around me, consuming anything else I heard. Even the tortured screams from the souls belonging to Hell were drowned out by the deep hum of these creatures.

Pain from sections all over my body increased as they sank their fangs into my flesh. I felt my knees buckle underneath me. I wasn't sure how many had attached themselves to me, but the weight was

162

becoming too much. I tried to cry out in frustration, but it was impossible to open my mouth the whole way. I thrashed my body back and forth angrily.

Sarenah, why? Why did this happen to me? I didn't know...

I ceased my movement for a second. Who had said that, and why had I been able to hear it? Besides the noise of the buzzing, my ears were completely covered up by layers upon layers of these spider-like creatures.

More twangs of pain filled my legs, my back, and my neck as they bit me repeatedly. I thrashed around madly now. I would *not* die like this. I yanked at the restraints on my wrists, trying to free myself from them. I needed use of my hands. I needed to pluck these horrible things off of me! I screamed out again, this time a desperate growl escaping my throat and echoing off the cold walls surrounding us, locking us inside.

A tiny hole was all I could see out of as the rest of my vision was completely blocked now. I saw movement in front of me as Saint tried to use his foot to kick away the spiders from my legs. He was just as covered as I was, his body a mound of large black insects, their legs dangling loosely once their teeth had found a place to latch onto. My heart sank. Of course Saint would be trying to save me even as the same devastating thing was happening to him.

My legs buckled again. I wouldn't be able to hold myself up much longer. This wasn't even a fair fight. I had been stripped of all angelic power, my sword had been taken and my hands were bound. I almost laughed. Of course, what was I expecting? This was Hell. Nothing was fair.

Will I ever get the privilege of seeing your face again?

And that's when it hit me. I felt like I couldn't breathe, and it wasn't because of these hideous leeches sinking their teeth into me every two seconds. I knew that beautiful, deep voice. Draco. There was no mistaking it now. How was I able to hear him? This had to mean he was close by. My chest ached. He was near, but I'd never be able to make it to him. I was about to die.

I'm here! I wanted to scream. *Draco, please, find me! I'm here!*

And then I didn't hear him anymore. The voice was gone. If it had only been a hallucination, it had soothed me in a time of despair. My vision was completely gone now. The darkness engulfed me. Pain surged up the side of my arm. The weight was just too much to take. I couldn't tell if my calves were burning from the bites or from the heaviness.

I tried to say Draco's name, but my mouth wouldn't budge, so I said it in my head.

Draco...

I had failed. It had been a mesmerizing, lovely moment I had spent with the dark creature. I had been instantly drawn to him, but I'd never be given the opportunity to learn why. How could I have been so stupid to want to come here? I should've known better, and to make things worse, I had dragged Saint and Tabian into my ploy. Though Tabian annoyed me, I still felt bad right now that he was experiencing the same things as me as they gnawed on me, sucked my blood and suffocated me all at the same time. Cruel is what it was. So this is what torture felt like.

I attempted to stand up straight one more time before stumbling and landing on the grimy floor below, the bodies of the spider-like creatures acting like a cushion against the fall. The burning sensation from the bites was everywhere. There was a deep bite in the back of my neck just then, one of the worst ones yet, when the buzzing ceased and the pain began to subside. I felt light again, like myself.

Someone cackled nearby, the sound bizarre. More people laughed.

I looked up. I could see again, and there were demonic eyes glowing red, dozens of them, staring in at us. They were on the other side of the door.

"We have an audience," I mumbled under my breath. Anger flashed through me. We had been their entertainment. And now all of the spider creatures had vanished. I looked down as the red welts caused by the bites, some of them still bleeding, started to heal.

"Someone's going to pay for that," Saint grumbled as he, too, slowly rose to his feet, his eyes narrowed and glaring at the eyes peering in, their amusement even more evident as their cackles grew louder at our fury.

I glanced over at Tabian as he inspected himself for injuries. He looked up then and met my glance. I nodded at him and some sort of understanding passed between us. He was stronger than I gave him credit for.

"What do we have here?" someone asked.

I looked out at the glowing eyes. They never blinked.

A dark creature pushed his way to the front so he was standing directly in front of the bars. He was hideous, his face covered in boils, his nose drawn up like a pig's. His fingers curled around the bars, revealing long, pointy claws.

"Who are you?" I asked, the last of my wounds disappearing.

Drool dripped from his mouth as he opened it to take a breath, his snout drawn upward even more by the movement.

"It doesn't matter who I am, Sarenah."

"How do you know who I am?"

He attempted a smile, but it came out as a snorting sound. "Everyone knows who you are, Sarenah."

I hated the way he said my name.

"You're in our domain now. Your strength has no purpose here. Why have you come?"

I started straight at him, my gaze never faltering. I would not back down to some lowlife trying to intimidate me. "I was promised to be taken to Draco."

The cackling stopped and there was silence before the creature answered. "Promises mean nothing in Hell, my dear angel."

*Dear angel...*Gag.

He snorted again and more drool dripped. "Draco is dead."

My heart plummeted at the words, but my stance never swayed and neither did my glare. "Lies."

The disgusting creature shrugged. "Believe what you want, but the fact still remains that he's gone." He licked his lips to stop more drool from pouring out of his mouth. "And now I get to decide what to do with you and your friends here."

168

A grunt came from Tabian. It took me off guard, and my eyes left the dark creature to look at him. He had a fierce look on his face.

Saint stepped up beside me and placed his hand on my shoulder. I didn't welcome the comfort.

"Never have we had the pleasure of welcoming angels to the dark kingdom." He snarled, the red eyes still glowing all around him from behind.

"You'll let us go if you know what's best for you," Saint threatened.

"Draco isn't dead!" I screamed out at him. "Take us to him *now!*"

The horrific creature made a gurgling sound with his mouth. Anytime I lashed out with emotion, it just added to his amusement.

I sprinted over to the bars and rammed them with my body, trying to release my agitation as well as let these demons know I meant what I said. The cackling returned. I breathed in and out heavily as the anger washed over me. I needed to compose myself. I stood up straight once again and looked back at Saint.

"We just need one measly opportunity..." he mumbled so low I barely heard it.

"I demand we speak with someone else!" I turned back to face the pig-like demon.

His tongue lapped at the edge of his snout. "There is no one else. I have been given permission to do with you as I please."

"Just need that door open an inch," Saint whispered in my ear.

I gritted my teeth together, ready to unleash my wrath on these foul creatures even if it meant without the use of my hands. "So, what is it you intend to do?"

"Hmmm..." He smacked his snout with his hand, making a disgusting snapping sound. He pressed a claw up against the side of his head as if in deep thought, pausing for a second. "I wonder what would happen to an angel if thrown into the flame of a fire..."

The snickering began all around him then.

"Three burnt angels..." He repeated the tapping motion with his claw on the side of his head. "Yes, yes. I like it very much. I wonder if we should start at

170

your wings first and make it a game...see if those beautiful features of yours shrivel up into little stubs on your back. Then we'll go from there. We'll burn you in sections."

These creatures were not only grotesque physically, their thoughts were so utterly demented that it made my stomach sick with even the thought that they would do something like that. I had to remind myself repeatedly that I wasn't on Earth anymore, that I truly was in a place where ultimate pain and suffering occurred.

"You didn't think we'd just leave you in that cell to bide your time. This isn't a luxury hotel, my dear angel. Everyone is especially excited, as you can tell I'm sure, about your arrival here. Angels as guests, and willing ones I might add..." His eyes shifted over to Saint. "It is a pity that Draco can't be here. I'm sure he would've loved to have been the one to destroy you himself." He attempted another smile which just wrinkled up his face more, his laughter coming out more like wheezing.

Saint pressed his face against the bar so that he was inches from the creature's snout. "If you try to hurt her, you'll have to deal with me."

"Only fools make threats they cannot keep."

The cackles resumed. It was like nails on a chalkboard. I was dying to make it stop.

The creature took a few steps back. "Take them to the fiery pits." And with that command, the door to our prison cell fell open. It was the opportunity Saint had been waiting for.

15

Draco

I felt the insanity start to take over. I knew the moment it happened as I heard the whisper in my head. It was strange, yet comforting the way it happened. The voice had been Sarenah's.

I'm here! Draco, please find me! I'm here!

Though brief, anguish washed over me as I clenched my fists together. This woman...*angel*, I corrected myself, had spoken to me. I knew it wasn't real, but it disturbed me in such a way as if she had been crying out to me. She had *needed* me. What was my warped mind trying to do to me? It was astonishing how my brain could remember every detail of how her voice sounded during our encounter. Her voice had been strong and steady even as a whisper. And then one more *Draco* and she had been gone. The way she said my name sent shivers crawling up my arms even now as I reminisced. What was it about this Sarenah? Why did she seem to be tormenting me so? Why did I now seem to have a thing for *angels?* I wanted to be disgusted by her, but attraction was even too mundane a word to describe exactly the way I was feeling right now. It was as though I were connected

174

to her somehow, even though that had been the first time I had even seen her. And the way she had cried out to me in my thoughts as if she needed me to save her drove me absolutely out of my mind with rage, rage against anyone that would dare try to hurt her. This was so out of character for me. I had been with plenty of women, both mortal and immortal, and none of them had had this effect on me, had gotten into my head and into my...heart. I wanted to laugh at the thought that a heart even existed within me. There may be an organ there, but a heart in the human sense, one that could be filled with emotions and dare I say it *love* had never crossed my thoughts before. I had barely even touched this angel, our fingers entwined, and our lips grazing each other's for merely a moment, so why was I so caught up in this Sarenah? What kind of power did she have over me? Had it all been a scheme to get me thrown into these dungeons?

You must be nearby. They're hiding you from me.

I clasped both hands over my ears and pressed hard against the sides of my head. I wanted to scream at the voice, at *her* voice, cursing it and demanding it get out of my head and leave me alone, but I knew better. They wanted me to suffer. That's why I was stuck here. Suffering was a game. The more of it I tried to shrug off as not bothering me, the better chance I'd have of them giving up on me, realizing I wasn't weak and releasing me. I had to push through this.

The moment the voice stopped again and I was relieved it was gone, I wanted it back. It was someone to talk to even if it just proved my sanity was slipping. I waited but there was nothing.

Sarenah, if you really needed me, I'd be there in a heartbeat.

I waited for some sort of response. I shook my head at what I was trying to do. I slapped myself alongside the head for giving in to the sweet voice of her memory.

They said you destroy angels.

I had been in many battles with angels over the centuries. Some had fallen at my hand. I bit my bottom lip.

I would protect you with my own life. I don't understand it myself. I don't understand any of this.

I wanted to sob in my hands, but my stubbornness took over and reminded me of how strong I was. Maybe I *did* belong in here. If Sarenah was standing here in front of me and needed protection, I would go against my own kind to save her. I really had crossed the line, and even though I hadn't known she was an angel at first, I did now and yet still I was clinging onto her.

I believe you.

Sarenah...

Draco...

I closed my eyes in anguish. *Don't go.*

I'm here.

But no, she really wasn't. They had found a weakness and gotten into my head. I should stop talking to myself, but it was too much of a temptation to overcome.

Why are you here?

For you. Such a simple answer.

I sighed. *I'm just a pawn used in an evil scheme.*

There was a hesitation before the voice answered. *We all have orders to follow, but right now I find myself following my own.*

177

We've crossed the line.

We'll endure it together.

I would be lying to myself if I didn't admit this gave me comfort. I should be trying to end it, but this I gave into.

They're going to try to kill me. Her voice was pleading, on the edge of desperation.

I closed my eyes and allowed my face to sink into my palms. *You have to fight.*

Oh, I will. I'll fight them all. They say you're dead. Close to it...

I opened my eyes. Someone was outside watching me. I stood and walked over to the bars. There were three demons cloaked in black, hoods over the heads, their faces shadowed. They were silent for a moment before whispering amongst each other again.

"What shall they do with him?"

"Can they not strip him of his power?"

"He looks weary, does he not?"

I narrowed my eyes, my hands gripping onto the bars tighter. "Speak to me!"

Their comments came in threes again.

178

"How will his power diminish?"

"We must keep him contained."

"His destruction is endless."

I trembled as the anger rose slowly through me, radiated up to my abdomen and continued to increase. They were peering in at me as if I was some sort of caged animal and ignored me as if I couldn't understand what they were saying. "I can hear your words," I told them, my tone low, on the edge.

"I am surprised at his agility after being here so long."

"Truly remarkable. They're having trouble finding ways to torture him."

"Everyone has a weakness. Everyone."

They blatantly ignored me, causing my irritation to burn like a raging fire from within.

Draco, where are you? You've left me. I need to hear your voice. You've gone.

I felt as though I couldn't take it anymore. I gripped onto the bars with one hand as my head slowly sank down toward the floor. I clenched my jaw together, feeling an overwhelming sense of grief and wrath balling up in the pit of my stomach. It climbed upward now in my throat as the three demons continued whispering to each other about me, in front of me, and the voice inside my head belonging to Sarenah echoed from behind. The madness hit me as the furious flames climbed higher in my neck. I could taste the flames now. I was going to lash out. My hand trembled against the bar, but I needed to hold myself steady.

"He's on the verge."

"That should be our sign."

"We must converse to the others."

And the rawness of this overwhelming fury burned my tongue. I brought my head back up. The demons had gone. My trembling ceased. I inhaled quickly and let the air back out slowly as I tried to calm my pulse. I sucked in a few more breaths before slowly turning and going back to the middle of the floor where I sat. Glancing toward the barred door, no one was there. It was just me and my thoughts.

A temporary interruption, Sarenah. I'm all yours again.

16

Cynda

I sat straight up in bed.

There it was again. I hadn't been dreaming. Someone was knocking impatiently on my door in the middle of the night.

I sucked in a deep breath before standing up and retrieving a fluffy gray robe from the back of a chair. The knocking grew louder. I pulled the robe around me as quickly as I could, my heart pounding in my chest as I hurried down the stairs.

I paused in front of the door. I had a horrible feeling that something was very wrong. *I probably shouldn't open this.* I hesitated. *I probably don't have a choice.*

I reached for the knob and swung the door wide open.

"Well, it's about time. It's pouring out there. I'm drenched." A tall, slender woman made her way into my house without invitation. She pulled back a black hood that was attached to a full-length black trench coat that glistened from the rain.

My suspicions were confirmed as she turned around and glared at me, irritation evident in her eyes. I ran a hand nervously through my short hair and closed the door. She reeked of evil, the foul smell from the underworld entering my nostrils. "What do you want?" I tried to keep my voice steady so she wouldn't see my nerves grabbing hold of me.

The demon folded her hands together in front of her, a smile now playing on her crimson lips. "You're needed in Hell."

And just like that, my peaceful Earth-bound life was shattered by a visitor in the night. I should've known they would come. I should've tried to hide. But where? They would've found me. My stomach sank. *Sarenah and Draco.* There would be no other reason for such an intrusion. "Where is she?"

Her pointy eyebrows shot up. "Who?"

"You know exactly who. Sarenah."

The demon flung her dark hair away from her shoulder. "None of this is your concern."

"You're making it my concern." I watched as her eyes pierced through me as if trying to read my thoughts.

"I was ordered to retrieve you." Her voice was low and steady but on the verge of losing her temper.

183

I tugged at the belt of the robe, making it even tighter. "Find someone else."

The demon flew over to me and put her face in front of mine, the stench coming from her pores nauseating. She was an inch from my face, our noses almost touching. "I *am* taking you with me." Her eyes then threatened me silently.

There was no way I was going to Hell without a fight. I had been there before, and I *never* wanted to go back. It was the type of experience that left one tainted. I knew after being there, seeing souls tortured, hearing their incessant groaning and smelling death, I'd never be the same woman I once had been. Then again, I was fairly certain not many, if any besides myself, had been given the opportunity to leave. My dreams were still turned to nightmares because of what my eyes had been forced to see. I shuddered.

"This doesn't make sense." I had to hold the demon off until I could figure out how to escape. My eyes frantically searched the room for some sort of magic I could use on her. "I haven't practiced witchery in a very long time. There's nothing I can do." What object could I use for a quick incantation? My lips moved slightly as I tried to recall the words of a spell. It had been so long. My anxiety increased. I needed to put this demon in a trance and get out of here.

"This matters to me not," she snapped, putting her hands on her hips impatiently. "I owe you no explanation."

"You do!" I exclaimed, knowing very well that upsetting a demon could be extremely dangerous, but she wasn't giving me any time to work a spell. She was being pushy, and I couldn't concentrate on a spell and focus on what she was saying without my anxiety compelling me to yell at her. "They can't expect me to just go without a reason as to why."

She gritted her teeth together. "This is them being nice, giving you the opportunity to go while still conscious." The demon shot another warning with her eyes. "You don't get a say in the matter."

My lips mumbled as a few words came back to me. I ran my hand over some knick-knacks that had been placed on a small table near the front door. No, none of these would do...

185

"Let's go," the demon insisted.

"Not yet," I whispered.

It was as if I could see actual flames coming to life from within her dark eyes.

"I want to go upstairs and change. You can't expect me to be wearing my pajamas and robe." I was hoping this would work as a stalling method.

"I don't care what you're wearing." She was furious with me.

"I'll just be a moment." I turned to go up the stairs. She was following closely behind. Something told me she wasn't going to let me out of her sight.

My fingers ran along the railing up the stairs as my eyes frantically searched for *something* I could use. What was that spell that could put mortals into a trance for days without them remembering anything? I was sure it would work on immortals, too. I couldn't remember! It had been too long. I was never going to be any use to them in Hell. I couldn't even save myself now.

Turning around slowly in the middle of the staircase, my eyes met with the demon's. She seemed to glow red as she already sensed my defiance. "Look, I'm just trying to tell you that I haven't really been a witch since...well, since I was sentenced to live out eternity on Earth. That was a long time ago. How do they expect me to do anything in the underworld without the knowledge of my spells?"

She narrowed her eyes. "I don't care what you claim you don't remember, *witch.*" She raised up her arm and pointed for me to continue walking. "If you don't remember, I'm sure there are ways of trying to pull the information from you." A smirk crossed her lips.

My stomach twisted into an even tighter ball. I couldn't think about the ways in which I could get tortured in Hell. Hearing everyone else get tortured had been enough for me. I had given it all up, locked it all away in the back of my mind and promised never to return to those dark days. There had to be some way out of this mess.

As I rounded the corner in the hallway on the second floor, trying to remember the spell, a memory came to mind instead...

It was during the time we had lived in the old village. We were dirt poor and struggling just to get one meal a day. There was a terrible drought throughout the land, and my parents, who were farmers, spent most of their time dwelling over the fact that our fields were filled with withered, shriveled plants and that most of our animals were starved and dying. They sat at home and drank moonshine, fanning themselves from the heat and telling my sisters and me to run off and try to stay out of their way. I was the youngest of four sisters. My older sisters were mischievous, and I hadn't even known they had been practicing black magic until one peculiar day.

They ran off across the fields. I hurried after them.

"Are you coming, Cynda?" Hilda hollered back at me. "Come on, hurry up! You won't want to miss this!"

I couldn't have been more than eight or nine years old at the time. I clutched my cloth doll in my right hand and tried to go faster.

My sisters ducked down behind a rotted, giant log on the ground. They pulled down hard on my arm so that I'd get lower. I was panting from the running and the heat as I watched them.

"Are you sure it's going to work?" Lorna asked. "Quit fidgeting, Cynda," she scolded me. "You're going to get us all caught and whipped."

"Of course it's going to work." Hilda grinned. She looked over at Maura and took her hand. They peeked up over the log.

I cautiously did the same. Over in the distance was old Farmer Draken. He was our neighbor, and from what I knew of him, a really nice man. He had lost his wife and kids to an illness long before I was ever born. He was walking around doing chores around his barn and whistling as he periodically stopped to say some words to his horse that was tied a few yards away.

"What are we doing here?" I whispered.

Lorna looked at me, her eyes telling me to shut my mouth and keep my head low. "She shouldn't be here."

189

"Oh, Lorna, she's fine. She's one of us," Hilda said, giving me a quick wink.

Lorna wrinkled her nose. "She's a little pain, and if it all goes wrong, I just know it'll be her fault."

I ignored Lorna. She had always been so bossy. "What? What is it? What are you going to do?" I glanced down at my doll momentarily and wiped a piece of dirt from her face.

"Put the stupid doll down," Lorna instructed.

I gave her an unsure look but felt reassured when Hilda nodded for me to listen to her.

"Now give me your hands," Lorna said.

I watched them take each other's hands and form a circle behind the log. Something didn't feel right about what they were doing.

"Look how hesitant she is!" Lorna glared at Hilda.

Maura frowned. "We need her."

"We don't," Lorna protested.

"It's the only way it'll work if she joins us," Hilda whispered. "Come on, little Cynda. You want to be part of your sisters, don't you?"

I slowly nodded my head. "But...I..."

Maura placed a finger to my lips to hush me. "Don't be afraid. It's like the most amazing magic you could ever imagine."

"Magic?" I asked them.

"You're the final piece to our puzzle. You complete us," Hilda said, her voice encouraging.

Farmer Draken tripped over something and began cursing. Maura snickered.

"What kind of magic are we doing?" I asked.

"We just need your energy. You don't have to do anything but take our hands and watch," Maura explained.

I raised my eyebrows. "Watch what?"

Hilda pointed above the log. "Farmer Draken."

"You're...not going to hurt him, are you?" I asked.

Something evil stirred within Lorna's eyes at the mere mention of such an idea.

"Of course not, silly," Hilda replied, laughing quietly. "Just see if we can get inside his head a little."

Maura held out her hands again. I was still reluctant. "If you say it's all right..." I whispered.

Lorna threw back her head in frustration. "Oh, just get over here, you little pest!"

Farmer Draken began to whistle again as I took Maura's hand on my left, Hilda's on my right. I watched as my sisters closed their eyes and their lips began to move. They weren't saying anything I could comprehend. Maura's and Hilda's grip tightened on my hands. I suddenly felt like I didn't want to be there. I wanted to pick up my doll and run away, go back to my mama. I tried to pull my hand away, but that made Maura only squeeze harder. My hands were beginning to hurt.

Out of the corner of my eye, I watched Farmer Draken. He had stopped what he had been doing and was standing near his horse now. He was staring out into the distance, his arms at his sides.

Suddenly his hands reached up and began pulling on his hair. He began shrieking as if in terrible agony. He raked his fingers over and over in his hair as if trying to pick something from his skull.

Hilda and Maura were now watching him, their mouths hanging slightly open at the sight. Lorna still had her eyes shut, her lips moving even faster.

The farmer's head thrashed back and forth so violently, I thought it was going to roll right off his shoulders. His entire body was shaking in tremors. His shrieks had changed to strange squeaks.

"Lorna," Hilda whispered. "Stop, Lorna, please."

I pulled my hands away from my sisters. They didn't try to stop me this time. We were all peeking up over the log, Lorna now watching along with us, her eyes seeming to enjoy the sight before us. What seemed like a normal morning had turned very peculiar. What had my sisters done to that poor man? Fear gripped me. A once very kind, completely coherent Farmer Draken now seemed...almost mentally ill. He arms now lay limp at his sides, his head hanging more to one side than the other. His eyes looked sunken, his gaze upward at the sky as he walked in little circles, his feet dragging along the ground as he did so.

"It worked, it worked, it worked," Lorna kept repeating.

"What did you do?" I asked her.

She glanced my way for only a moment. "You mean, what *we* did," she corrected me. "Even you did this, little Cynda."

"Me? I don't even know what happened..."

"It doesn't matter," Maura interrupted. "We're sisters. We feed off each other's energy. This was a powerful spell. Without you, we wouldn't have been able to do it."

"But look at him," I whispered. "He looks..."

"Dizzy?" Lorna almost burst out laughing but quickly covered her mouth.

Hilda patted my knee. "It's okay, Cynda. We just wanted to try it. He won't be like this forever."

"He won't?" I watched the farmer continue to go in circles as if they had stripped his mind of all sanity.

Hilda shook her head. "It's temporary."

"Promise?" I asked.

Lorna rolled her eyes. "You are such a baby."

No one said anything else for a few minutes. Farmer Draken stumbled into his horse a few times. He seemed to be mumbling something now. The horse let out a displeased snort. This happened several times until he found himself at the back end

194

of the horse. To my horror, the horse suddenly raised up on his front legs and kicked its back legs out, the hooves making contact with Farmer Draken's head. It looked like the blow had made the man's head twist around as he fell over limp on the dusty ground.

Tears welled up in my eyes at what I had just seen.

"The horse...it got spooked by him. It just kicked him..." Hilda's eyes seemed filled with shock.

The tears were streaming down my cheeks now.

"Should we go see if he needs help?" Maura asked.

"No," Lorna snapped. "He's dead. Just let things be." She was still staring at him.

"We have to go," Hilda whispered. "We have to get out of here."

Lorna tore her eyes from the scene to glare at me. "Cynda, you will not say a word of this to anyone, do you hear?"

I looked up at her blankly. I shouldn't have just seen what I did. No one should've.

"If you do," Lorna continued. "The same thing that happened to Farmer Draken will happen to you."

The threat was enough to send me running as fast as I could back toward my house. I wasn't going to be the slow one now. I let fear carry me away.

That was the first time I had ever witnessed witchcraft. That had been the trance spell that I needed right now to confuse this demon. If only my sisters were here with me, they'd be able to help. They had taught me everything I knew. We had nothing better to do with our time than to invoke things that should've been left be.

Sadness washed over me as I thought about my sisters and how much I missed them now. It had been awhile since I had even thought of them.

"Just give me a minute." I turned around to face the demon again. "I need to go to the bathroom. You don't need to watch me pee, do you?"

She continued to glare at me. "Hurry up. I'll be timing you."

There was no doubt in my mind that she would be timing me down to the very last second. I got into the bathroom and shut the door. I looked over the different things in the room. It was no use. I couldn't use any of these things. My eyes rested on the window. There was a roof underneath it. It would be a tricky jump, but it was better than the alternative.

The window squealed out in protest in the cold air as I pried it open. My heart pounded in my chest at the thought of how little time I had. I wiggled my body through the small opening and flopped down to the roof below, the leathery green canvas slippery from the rain. My leg bent in an awkward way underneath me. I cringed but managed to roll over the roof and plop down not-so-gracefully on the hard, cold ground. Standing up, I glanced up at the window. Not seeing her face, I began to run as fast as I could down the street. It was the middle of the night. No one was in sight. It didn't matter. No one would be able to help me now, anyway.

I turned a corner. My lungs felt like they were on fire. When had been the last time I'd exercised? I may be immortal myself, but I was still not young in human years by any means.

I had just hesitated a moment to catch my breath when something caught the back of my legs. I fell down face-forward, biting my tongue as my jaw hit the ground. Blood filled my mouth. I struggled to turn

197

around, but I already knew the demon had caught me.

Her eyes seemed to glow in fury and she was still clinging to my ankles with a fierce grip. "You'll pay for that, *witch.*"

I groaned from the aches that already filled my body from the torture I had just inflicted upon myself from my failed attempt at escape. I should've known better, but if I hadn't tried, I would've kicked myself later.

"You're time's up. You're coming now." She pressed her hand to the ground beside us. It seemed to melt away and transform into a portal to Hell.

This was it. There was nothing I could do now to save myself. "Please...just please tell me that Sarenah is okay."

"This has nothing to do with her," the demon snarled.

The portal widened.

"Who then? Tell me who."

She glared at me one more time before grabbing me by the wrists. "Rebecca."

17

Saint

My hands were no longer bound. The restraints had vanished. They were getting ready to take us to some fiery pits to torture us. I knew this had been the opportunity I had been waiting for. As soon as the door opened even the slightest creak, I took off as fast I could and charged through as I fought the ugly shadows with my bare fists.

A large quantity of them backed up. I had taken them by surprise with my sudden agility. I had to get us out of this mess. This wasn't going to be how I ended up fading away. No, not like this. These creatures disgusted me, and Draco disgusted me even more. I used my anger as fuel as a dark creature rushed toward me. A blow with my fist colliding with its head sent it soaring backward.

"What are you idiots doing?" the one that had been speaking to us bellowed out. "Get him!"

The dark creatures were known for their evil ways, their delight to see others in anguish, but they were also cowards, afraid to get harmed themselves. It took a moment for their leader's words to sink into their measly little brains before they started to crowd around me.

"Heads up!" Sarenah yelled.

She tossed heavy links of chain through the air. I barely had time to catch it before the shadows were on me. I swung with all my might, still using the anger at the situation to give me added strength. I could hear chains clanging from behind me. I was sure Sarenah and Tabian were putting up a good fight of their own. I was worried about her and wanted to look back, but I knew one glance away from these things could send me straight to my end.

How could Draco have touched Sarenah like that? I swung the chain back and let it sway forward with its own weight. It made contact with several shadows, many of them falling to the floor and dissipating into nothing. I knew that meant I had completely destroyed them. I had seen that happen many times in battle with a slice of my sword. Oh, how I wished I had my sword now. I wasn't used to having to battle without it in my hand.

I could hear Sarenah struggling. It forced me to turn my back to a large group of shadows. One of them was gripping onto the back of her head, pulling at her hair. She was reaching back, trying to rip it off of her. I grabbed it by the neck and squeezed. It cried out in pain as I threw it toward more creatures coming at me. Sarenah met my glance momentarily before returning to the fight.

We were holding them off, but there were just so many of them. We were completely outnumbered, and I was already tiring myself out. It was only a matter of time. We had to do something, and fast. I glanced over my shoulder. I didn't want to do it, but I wanted selfishly to get out of here in one piece, and I was taking Sarenah with me. That left only one logical choice. Tabian. He'd have to act as our decoy.

I felt like a lowlife the moment the thought entered my mind, but I didn't have time to waste on how I felt. I had to focus on getting away from these foul things so we could find a way out.

I moved quickly to Sarenah and reached for her hand. I didn't look at her face to see her reaction. I just gripped on tightly and moved past Tabian whose back was to us as he swung a lantern at several creatures trying to capture him. We were rushing down a dark hall, leaving Tabian behind.

"What about Tabian?" Sarenah hissed from my side. "Saint, no..."

I squeezed her hand harder. "We have to keep moving." I knew what I had done was spineless. I had never left behind a fellow angel before. Then again, I had never been fighting for my life in the pits of Hell.

18

Tabian

I tossed the lantern forward by its long handle. It hit another shadow who fell back against those behind it. These creatures acted slowly. It seemed like their method of attack was jumping on their prey. You could easily shake one or two, but when you had many of them on you, you were in trouble.

I had turned around to see Saint and Sarenah slip by. My heart sank at the thought that I had become bait. I released the negative feelings as another shadow approached me. He fell back. The creature with the pig's snout had disappeared. That probably wasn't a good thing. Who knows what kind of horrific evils he was gathering up to come after us...

My thoughts turned to the conversation I had overhead between Sarenah and Saint. Was my assumption correct that she wasn't after Draco because she wanted him dead and gone but because she was...in love with him? It just didn't seem possible. How could Sarenah claim she had feelings for something that belonged down here in Hell? I was sure Draco had committed countless acts of terrible things, including murder. She would know this about him, so what was it that had happened between them? It was hard for me to stomach the thought that a beautiful angel like Sarenah had succumbed to the charms of an immoral creature such as Draco. And why would Saint be helping her if he knew these things? He seemed just as infatuated with her as I. It just didn't add up.

A shadow jumped on my back. It sent me stumbling backward and into a wall. The motion seemed to cause it to release its grip on me. I stood back up. The shadows were everywhere surrounding me. I was at a dead end with nowhere to run. I could see some of them flying over my head now. They were closing in.

A pang of jealousy ripped through me as I saw Sarenah and Saint hand in hand, their forms vanishing into the darkness as they tried to make a run for it. It was no use. They wouldn't escape. None of us would get out of this. It had been a death trap the moment we took the leap into that black hole. I tried to hold my head up high. A shadow jumped down from overhead and landed on my back. It made a screeching sound in my ear. All I ever wanted was to be Sarenah's hero, the one she depended on to protect her. I just wanted her to recognize me as an equal and not for a little twerp that followed her around like a stalker. My love for her knew no limitations, and if this is what it took to prove to her how I felt, for her to know I was doing this to save her, then so be it.

Another shadow jumped on me and then another. The handle of the lantern was forced out of my hand as I buckled to my knees, the jagged floor cutting into my skin. This was it. I waited for the darkness to consume me and relieve me of my sadness.

A loud roar echoed through the corridor. It came again, this time the entire floor quaking beneath me. The shadows screeched out in fear and hurried to scurry away. I was able to stand now, the area completely void of any creatures except myself. Another roar sounded. I clenched my fingers into my palms, knowing whatever was the cause of that noise was not going to be as small as the shadows. In fact, I was pretty sure that it was going to be monstrous looking. My legs felt like jelly, but I still managed to get them working again as I took off in the opposite direction of the noise, hoping Saint and Sarenah weren't too far down.

There were no lanterns here. The blackness could be leading me to anywhere really, but I still ran as fast as I could, my arms out in front of me as braces so I wouldn't smack face first into a wall and knock myself out.

"Tabian!"

It was Sarenah, and she wasn't far ahead.

"I'm coming!" I yelled out to her.

"Hurry!"

The floor was shaking underneath me. I knew whatever was chasing after me would soon be on top of me.

I saw an archway up ahead, Saint and Sarenah standing there waiting for me. I wanted to lash out at them for leaving me, but there was no time for that now.

"What is that sound?" Sarenah asked, her face looking paler than usual as the same thoughts about something hideous headed our way must have been running around in her mind.

I tried to compose myself, remain calm for her sake. "Whatever it is, all the shadows ran away from it."

We stepped further into a lit room made entirely of rock. There was nothing in the room, and the only way out was to go up. There was no ceiling, and it was as high as I could see leading up to somewhere else. If only we could fly, but my wings seemed sluggish and wouldn't work. It was another dead end.

I looked up to see Saint's eyes. They were large in alarm. He was staring at something behind me. Fear seized me. I slowly turned around. There was the creature who had made the roar and scared all the shadows away. It was huge, almost wolf-like as I peered up at it, massive fangs protruding down over its bottom lip. The eyes glowed green and didn't seem to have pupils. Most of its fur was missing as if it were a diseased animal. A hellhound. It opened its mouth and let out another roar, its hot, foul breath filling my nostrils. I took a step back.

"What do we do?" I asked aloud.

"You surrender," the grotesque creature answered. "Defiance will not be tolerated here and will only make your suffering greater."

I looked back at Saint and Sarenah. They remained silent.

"Now move!" the creature yelled, its voice deep and raspy. It stepped to the side so I could walk past it and head back in the direction we had come. I cringed at the thought of having to get too close to it, patches of missing fur combined with seeping wounds on its side.

I went first. Sarenah and Saint were close behind me followed by the hellhound as we stepped back into the blackness. My heart sank again as I heard Sarenah whisper, "Please don't let go of my hand, Saint."

19

Cynda

"Where are you taking me?" I asked the demon. I was walking in Hell, in my bare feet and fluffy gray robe nonetheless. I was scared, yes, but my irritation was growing with the mere mention of the name of Rebecca. I had never known what had become of her. She was the sweetest, most precious girl. She had been caught up in the scheme of things and had suffered for it. When I had seen Sarenah as an angel, I had assumed Rebecca had also become one. Now I wasn't so sure.

"To the counsel."

I wanted to curl up in a ball and cover my ears. There were the groans again, the voices of those suffering calling out to me. They were in everlasting flames all around me like walls. I couldn't feel the heat from them fortunately, but I knew the poor souls inside of them could. I knew they probably deserved to be here, but it didn't mean I didn't feel bad for them. They reached out at me with their arms as I passed by. There was nothing I could do but try to ignore them. Hell was their destination.

"If they think I'm going to do anything to hurt Rebecca, you'd better tell them otherwise. I'd rather die."

The demon turned around and glared at me, her hair shimmering from the illumination of the flames. "That is no concern of yours right now."

Yeah, right. *Everything* was my concern. I was about to be poked and prodded mentally by those designated able and capable to do so, those who had gone through the ranks to make it to counsel, who had probably done terrible, dreadful things to be considered the best of the best. Oh, how I missed my comfy bed at home!

We were in an open area on top of a cliff. I glanced down at my bare toes covered in red sand and sighed. There were chairs placed near the edge of the cliff and five hooded creatures. I was grateful they were hooded. Who knows what kind of hideous faces lay underneath...

"Here she is, the *witch.*" The demon gave me a push from behind, making me take a few steps closer to them.

I loved how she emphasized the fact that I was a witch. Wasn't it obvious that's why they had chosen me? I suppose it didn't take much intelligence to be a demon.

"Come forward," one of the counselors commanded.

I chewed on the inside of my lip and cautiously approached them. There was no chair for me to sit on. I felt the aches in my strained muscles and then tried to ignore the fact that at my age, I had just tried to outrun an outraged demon.

I stood there feeling very vulnerable. I felt as if I could almost cry because of where I was, but I wouldn't give them the satisfaction of knowing I could be weak. Evil used vulnerabilities as weapons against you.

"You're Cynda?" one of them asked.

I folded my hands together in front of me. "That's me."

"We have heard rumors about your abilities as a powerful witch. Tell us, what is it you can do? Are there limitations to your magic?"

I turned to see where the female demon had gone. She wasn't here anymore. I took a deep breath. "It has been years, hundreds of years to be exact, since I've used any magic."

One of the counselors roared out, the hood of his cloak coming slightly off his head, revealing greenish-colored skin. "Was that the question I asked of you? Was it?"

Wow, they had really short tempers. I was going to have to think very carefully about what I said to them. Then again, I'd be pissed off if I called Hell my home, too. "No."

"I don't care how long it's been since you've practiced being a witch. You're not going to stand there and tell us that you have no recollection of your power, of what you did." He paused for a moment. "And you know exactly what it was that you did."

I swallowed hard as I thought of what to say. "I was merely the teacher."

"Answer the question, and don't make me repeat myself." He pulled the cloak back down over the exposed skin to hide it.

"There are always limitations."

215

"Such as?"

I shrugged. "Depends on the situation."

He roared again.

"You can be displeased with my responses all you want, but you've asked me to answer them, and I am. I can't stand here and tell you a witch's spell knows no boundaries, because the fact of the matter is it does."

"What is the most accounted for limitation?"

I wanted to roll my eyes but refrained. Relentless evil bastards. I thought for a moment before saying, "Interferences."

The counselors began mumbling amongst each other. I couldn't understand what it was they were saying.

"Elaborate."

"Okay..." I began playing with the edges of my fingernails. "If I'm in the middle of a spell, an interference could be my own state of mind, if I'm not totally focused on what I'm doing. An interference could be someone getting in the way of the spell physically and trying to put an end to it. It could be the mental state of the person you're trying to crack.

There are barriers and things that can get in the way. It happens...happened all the time."

"How did she do it?"

I raised my eyebrows. "She?"

"Sarenah."

The name struck a nerve with me. Like Rebecca, I would always protect Sarenah. No amount of mental or physical torment would ever change that. I wished I could get a better read on these despicable creatures, what their intentions were for all this questioning. What was going on with Sarenah? I knew some sort of plan was taking place around me, but I needed to figure out how I fit into the equation and try to put an end to it all before it got out of hand, before it was an end to us all.

I let the question repeat in my thoughts. *How did she do it?* It was like déjà vu from a lifetime ago when my powers were the strongest. Those who were against me I crushed, and I had truly felt my powers had no limits back then. The townspeople were simple-minded fools. I disregarded them as nothing more than insects as they looked down their noses at me and my sisters.

Instead of immortal evil creatures, my sisters and I were standing in front of humans who were our judge and jury. We had unleashed havoc upon their town, our town that we had grown up in. They were trying to put an end to us.

I was a scraggly, thin woman who had felt out of place her entire life, but now, in front of these people, the situation was empowering. They were going to try to burn my sisters and me at the stake. I couldn't shake the smile from my face. If they only knew what I could do to them...

I was bound by rope and tied to a pole. My sisters, Hilda, Lorna, and Maura, were likewise bound, each to their individual pole. These men thought they could intimidate us. They wanted answers for the darkness that had crept over their town, thinking that we'd talk if they said they'd spare our lives. We knew better. They'd kill us anyway.

"Where is Sarenah?" one man asked.

A crowd from town was gathering around us now. I looked each of them in the eye as they came. "I don't know." But I did know. She was keeping Draco away until it was safe.

"How did she do it?" someone shouted out. "What kind of black magic have you been teaching our girl?"

Oh, yes. They thought Sarenah was *their* girl. My sisters and I were the outcasts, but little did they know how interested Sarenah was in getting away from here.

"I don't know how she did it," I replied calmly, my smug smile still glued on my face. "It's a mystery even to me."

"This is blasphemy, what you've done! You and your sisters will die and pay for your sins!"

Idle threats from pea-brain townspeople. They wanted me to break down and sob when the spell was already being conjured up in my mind, one that would destroy them all.

"You must ask forgiveness, child!" a woman called out.

I recognized her from the market. She was homely and plump. She should be asking forgiveness. She was busy stuffing her face while my sisters and I starved. She was the portrait of hypocrisy.

"I'm not sorry for what I've done!" I shouted back to her.

She looked shocked I would say such a thing.

"After all," I continued. "It was the most wondrous thing I've ever laid eyes on!"

My sisters burst into laughter at my side.

"Are you sure, Cynda?" Hilda asked me quietly. "Are you sure you can pull this off?"

I glanced her way and gave her an assuring nod. "You have nothing to worry about tonight, sister."

Hilda grinned.

"Wondrous? It's destroyed our town, killed our people!" A man with a burning torch made his way to the front of the crowd. "It could destroy the whole world."

I stared at him for a moment, taking the scene in. The air smelled like rain around us. "This is true, but you can't deny the beauty of it all."

"She's insane!" a woman yelled out.

"They all are!"

"Light the fires!"

The man moved closer with the torch, his eyes burning into mine. My lips began mumbling the spell.

220

"She's trying something!" someone hollered out. I could sense the fear in her voice.

You should be afraid, I thought momentarily before resuming my focus on the spell.

"Hurry, Cynda!" Maura hissed.

"You're distracting me," I mumbled to her, my eyes still closed.

The man with the torch walked over to Maura first and lit the hay piled at the bottom of the pole. She cried out as the smoke quickly turned into flames.

I finished the spell and opened my eyes. I looked over at Maura, the flames climbing higher now, reaching her ankles. She stared at me, terror evident on her face.

Why hadn't it worked? Panic seized me.

I began chanting in my mind again, this time with more force as I tried not to let Maura's screams ruin my focus. My lips moved furiously.

More shrieking jolted me out of my trance. I looked over to find Hilda's pole now lit. I couldn't even see Maura anymore as the flames covered her entire body. I looked out in the crowd, my eyes large

221

now with fear. No! They were seeing my terror. I had promised myself they wouldn't see me afraid, but I was in full-blown panic myself. I didn't understand.

"Cynda!" Lorna cried out as they moved to her next.

Something was wrong. I was stronger than ever, so it couldn't be the spell. No. These people were being helped, but by who?

My eyes scanned the crowd once more, tears streaming down my cheeks from knowing my sisters were dying beside me and there was nothing I could do to stop it.

Why had I been so cocky? Why hadn't we just run away with Sarenah and Draco? I shouldn't have even bothered with trying to get revenge on this stupid town.

Then I saw her.

She moved to the front of the crowd, her eyes meeting mine.

"Rebecca," I whispered.

She was as beautiful as ever, a teenage girl who harvested such goodness inside her. Her long blonde hair and white dress were fluttering in the wind, her blue eyes illuminated by the flames of my burning sisters. I knew in that moment that she had done this. She had blocked my spell. There was no one else strong enough. But why?

The man turned around and looked at her as if waiting for her order. He was standing beside me now, my three sisters silent. I knew they were dead and gone. Here I was, tied to this pole, waiting for my turn.

"Let her down," Rebecca told him.

There were cries of protest behind her.

"You're sure?" the man asked. "She's the worst one."

"No, she's not." Rebecca glanced my way again. "She's the only one that has any goodness within her. The others, they were evil."

I knew she was referring to my sisters.

"What will happen to her?" a woman shouted out. "Will she run loose in our town?"

Rebecca shook her head. "No. You'll never see her again. She has others to answer to."

I watched her disappear into the crowd as the man released my restraints.

223

I let the memory drift away, leaving me feeling melancholy as I looked up at the counselors before me.

"No one knows how she did it, not even Sarenah," I answered them.

"That's impossible!" one of the other counselors bellowed out.

Nothing I could tell them would make them happy. I didn't have the answers they sought. "You can't expect me to tell you something I don't know myself. I tell you the truth. It was the most amazing, terrifying thing that anyone has ever witnessed, but we don't know how it came to be."

"What were the intentions of the spell?"

I sighed. Dredging these memories up left me feeling exhausted. "The intention of the spell was simply to create something to protect Sarenah."

"Protect her how?"

"I was going for an object such as an amulet to wear around her neck. It would have the power of protection locked within it. The amulet would feed off of Sarenah's fear. When she was afraid, it would essentially create a shield around her."

"You could've created such a thing?"

I shrugged. "I didn't really get a chance to try. Something went wrong with the spell..."

"Obviously!" one of them shouted out.

I kept my composure as they continued to have outbursts of anger. I had to remind myself where I was and how common these reactions were here. It had been a while since I had thought about all of these people from my past. I had dealt with my sentence of being Earth-bound forever. I had tried to resume some sort of normalcy in my life. I had always suspected that things would cycle out again, but it hadn't happened in such a long time, that my anticipation had faded. Ironically, it had hit me when I had least expected it, sleeping and warm in my own bed. I wondered now what would've happened if I had never unlocked my door. Surely the demon would've broken it down in search of me.

"I thought you were the teacher," one of them remarked.

I nodded. "Correct. I was teaching Sarenah the spell. She wanted to do it herself."

"How much magic had you taught her?"

I thought for a moment. "None other than that. She had no interest other than protecting herself." I had liked Sarenah from the moment she boldly strolled through my door telling me she had heard I could *make things happen.* We had become instant friends, something I hadn't expected from someone as popular as her among the townspeople.

"You knew, didn't you, Cynda?" One of them stood now and walked over to me. I tried to make sure I was standing up straight. "You knew this would happen again."

I looked into the shadowed face within the dark hood. "I suspected it, yes."

"Why? What went wrong?"

I swallowed. I was never good at thinking before I spoke, and this created quite the challenge to me to not piss off counselors of Hell. "Their love is unnatural. The force behind such a love is unknown. All they had to do was see each other. That's what went wrong. Someone didn't do their job and keep Sarenah and Draco from crossing paths."

My words made quite the commotion amongst the counselors. They were outraged. Someone had slipped up on their end, and they knew it. I merely confirmed it for them.

The female demon that had awakened me from my sleep appeared again. She was standing too close for comfort.

"What should I do with her?" the demon asked them.

The counselor that had been standing near me turned to face me, and with a swift motion of his arm, slammed his fist into the side of my face. The force sent me stumbling backward into the demon who uttered her disgust as I collapsed at her feet wincing from the pain.

"Take her away to the chambers," he ordered. "Have her beaten."

20

Cynda

"Cynda, wake up."

My eyelids fluttered for a moment. Had I just heard someone?

"Cynda."

I groaned. I didn't want to be awake. In fact, right now, I didn't want to be alive. My entire body throbbed from the endless strikes I had received from the female demon who successfully carried out her orders to beat me.

The floor beneath me was hard and cold. My swollen lip stuck to the rock and I yelped out in pain as I made an attempt to sit up.

"Oh, you poor thing."

One of my eyes was swollen shut. The other one slowly opened. I felt so weary. When my eyes focused, I gasped.

Hilda grinned. "You've changed, sister."

"You mean she's old," Lorna chimed in.

It was my sisters! All three of them! They were here and speaking to me.

"Am I dead?" I whispered.

"Should be by the looks of you," Lorna remarked.

A small chuckle escaped my throat. They looked wonderful, maybe a little too vibrant. "Am I hallucinating?"

"No, Cynda, we're here," Hilda assured me. "We're really here with you."

"We've been given permission to come," Maura explained.

I struggled to sit up more. A sharp pain darted through the middle of my head.

"Take it easy, sister." Hilda put her hand on my shoulder and helped me steady myself. "You've been through a bad spell with that demon."

"She really got the best of you," Maura said.

I was sure I looked as bad as they all said I did. "Well, I didn't put up a fight. I mean, what's the use of fighting a demon?"

Maura nodded. "It would've only made things worse."

"You were always the smart one." Hilda flashed another smile.

Lorna looked away as she mumbled, "Yeah, smart enough to escape getting burnt at the stake."

When I didn't think I could feel any more pain than I already did, Lorna struck a nerve and sent my heart filling with a familiar ache. "I understand if you're mad at me. All of you."

"We're not mad." Maura bit her bottom lip. "The spell just didn't work."

I sat in silence for a moment as I focused on my breathing. The ache in my chest eased slightly. "You three have been here all this time, haven't you?"

They nodded their heads.

"Where else would the souls of wicked witches go?" Lorna stated.

I knew she was right. I had always assumed they'd gone to Hell, but I had never wanted to admit it to myself. I didn't want the guilt of lying awake at night while still being on Earth and knowing that my three beautiful sisters were in the underworld being tortured. It hadn't been fair. It was a guilt that had worn me down over the years.

"But then again, "Lorna continued. "Your soul was spared, dear sister." She eyed me, suspicion evident in her stare.

I pressed my lips together, the movement awakening pain in my mouth, reminding me that I had an injury there. "You think the spell I uttered was one to save myself, don't you? It really pains me to know that you've thought that all these years."

"Well, tell us what we *should* think then." Lorna clasped her hands together.

"I did the spell exactly as I should've," I told them. "I'm so sorry." I felt a lump grow large and thick in my throat. "I promised all of you it would work, that we'd be able to destroy those against us."

"It's okay." Hilda offered me her hand, which I took into mine. "We don't blame you."

"Speak for yourself," Lorna snapped.

Typical Lorna. She had always been on a rampage. She hated the world and everything in it. She had been, by far, the most dangerous of us all. She would create spells in fits of anger and annihilate anyone that crossed her.

"You can tell us what happened now if it'll make you feel better," Maura said softly.

I nodded my head. "I have been wanting to tell all of you that it wasn't my fault. The spell was

232

powerful. It should've worked. All of those people should have burst into flames themselves instead of you..."

"But?" Lorna asked.

I looked up at her and then away. Her jabs had always stung even when we were little girls. She was well aware of that fact, too. "The spell was blocked. Rebecca..."

"Rebecca?" Lorna gasped.

Hilda and Maura's brows furrowed.

"I should've known..." Lorna's gaze went off into the distance.

"This makes total sense now," Hilda said.

"It does?" Lorna asked. "How so? Why did she give Cynda the privilege of living?"

"Lorna," Maura scolded. "Rebecca hated us. She didn't hate Cynda. Tell her, Cynda."

Tears filled my eyes as I shook my head in agreement. "Yes," I whispered. "I do believe that is why I got to live."

"Well, you look horrible." Lorna glared at me.

"Lorna!" Hilda scolded.

I pressed my fingers to a sore spot on the side of my head. There was an open gash there seeping fluid. "Why were you allowed to come see me?"

The three of them exchanged glances.

"I mean, you didn't think I thought you were just visiting, right? I'm not that naive. Every nice gesture in a place like this has a purpose." I watched them look at me in acknowledgement. "Just spit it out, get it over with. What's your purpose here?"

Hilda cleared her throat. "We've come to ask for your help."

"Okay..."

Maura frowned. "In trying to stop the cycle from repeating itself."

"Sarenah's seen Draco," I spit out.

"What do you know of it?" Lorna asked right away.

"Have you spoken to her? What'd she say?" Maura then asked.

"What happened between them?" Hilda added.

I looked at each of them individually, studying them. Something was off. They had rambled off those questions too quickly. Their eagerness wasn't

234

characteristic of them, not in this way. I decided to test the waters by feeding into their curiosity. "I'm sure she's gone off to find him. Their connection would be too strong, too overwhelming for her not to follow through with it."

"Did she tell you that?"

"Did she say where she was going to find him?"

"How can we put an end to this? Tell us, sister, what's the key?"

I let my eyes close. My heart sank. Of course I would've been so easily fooled. They had broken me down physically just to be comforted by my sisters. They were trying to get information out of me on Sarenah and Draco, the cycle, if I knew of a way to make it all go away. These were not my sisters. These were demon replicas. They had put on a good show, I'd give them that. Even Lorna's moodiness had been copied, but she was never the first one to spit out a question like that. No, these were all too eager demons. Their excitement had given them away. And the sadness and guilt returned to me. My real sisters still didn't know I hadn't abandoned them with some spell that night. Their souls were still being tormented.

I swallowed back the lump and looked up at them. It was good to see their faces even if it wasn't real. "Can I ask all three of you something?"

Lorna rolled her eyes. "What is it?"

"That day the farmer died, when we were just kids, what was it that killed him?" I asked.

They remained silent, each of them exchanging glances again.

Their nervousness amused me. "You do remember, don't you?"

Maura let out a small chuckle. "Of course, we do."

"Remind me again what it was then," I urged her.

There was no response this time. Then all three of my sisters' lovely faces vanished into thin air and the suffocating guilt they left behind lingered within me.

"Get up," a voice said from behind me.

I felt sick to my stomach when I saw the female demon who had ruthlessly hit me again and again.

"Relax," she mumbled. "I'm not here for that."

"Then what?"

236

"I'm taking you to see someone."

"Who?"

The demon smirked. "Rebecca."

I suddenly felt short of breath. "What?"

The demon seemed pleased with my response. "Oh, yes, *witch,* we have her. And this is no illusion either."

Surely it couldn't be true. Rebecca couldn't be in Hell. She was too...pure. She had to have become an angel, I was sure of it.

"Get up and follow me or I'll drag you there by your hair," she threatened.

I somehow climbed to my feet against my body's protest and followed her out of the chamber and down a large staircase made of brass, our footsteps sounding heavy and echoing with each step.

This place we were going felt more like a home than what I had experienced here before. There were carpets underneath my toes now and furniture. The demon stopped in front of a room covered in windows. Peering in, I couldn't believe what I saw. There was Rebecca, still a pretty, young girl dressed in a cotton white dress, her blonde hair tied back in a satin blue bow.

"I don't believe it," I mumbled. "Surely this isn't the real Rebecca you're showing me. This is just another trick."

The demon chuckled. "Think what you want, but I assure you, this is Rebecca. She's been with us for a very long time. Go in, and figure it out."

"Figure it out?" I repeated.

"You know what I'm saying," she snapped. "She hasn't spoken a word to anyone since she's come here. Get her to talk. Get her to talk about Sarenah and what she knows."

She gave me a little shove forward and my hand clumsily landed on the doorknob. I opened the door and stepped foot inside. It was like a beautiful, spacious apartment, only it had more of a trapped feeling to it. I shut the door behind me and quietly made my way over to Rebecca's side. She seemed to notice me then and turned her head. Her eyes were full of sadness, and I knew then that this had to be real. They had taken Rebecca captive, but why? Why was this allowed to happen to her of all people?

"Rebecca," I whispered. I wanted to touch her, take her hand, anything to comfort her, but I wasn't sure if she even knew who I was. I stared at her angelic face for a moment. "Rebecca, do you know who I am?"

She nodded her head slowly.

"Who am I, then?"

I wondered if she'd speak to me. The demon said she hadn't spoken since she got here, so that could've meant hundreds of years of silence.

She glided her hand over mine just then and gave me a soft smile. Here she was comforting me when all I wanted to do was latch onto her and let her know it would be okay even though I wasn't sure it would be.

"Of course I know who you are, Cynda."

So she did know how to speak.

"They've brought me here to speak with you for some reason. Do you have any inclination as to why?" I asked her.

She pointed up just then. I followed the gesture to where there should've been a ceiling but none existed. It just climbed higher and higher into darkness. "You have to be very quiet. They're always watching, always listening."

I nodded understanding. This would not be a private conversation.

"And to answer your question, yes, I believe it has to do with my sister."

"Yes, that's right. Something's going on with Sarenah."

Sarenah and Rebecca had been extremely close. They only had a year age gap between them. Sarenah was a dark-haired beauty of seventeen, and Rebecca was all blonde curls and sweet eyes at sixteen. They stuck by each other's side through everything. Then Draco had separated them.

"I was sentenced to Earth for eternity. Sarenah became an angel." I saw Rebecca's face light up in relief at this information. "But you, why aren't you in Heaven?"

Rebecca sighed then, her eyes looking upward again before returning to my face. "They didn't know what to do with me."

"What do you mean?"

"The elements, neither good nor bad, they couldn't decide, so it was agreed upon I'd stay here."

"I don't understand why you were locked away..."

"Locked away but still taken care of," she added. "They've been prodding me lately. I haven't spoken to them. I knew something must've happened with Sarenah. What's happened? Do you know?"

I shook my head. "Not entirely. On Earth, Sarenah and I crossed paths. She was surprised I could see her. She's seen Draco..."

Rebecca let her head slump. "Oh." She rubbed a wrinkle out of the front of her dress. "Then that explains everything. It's beginning again."

"Yes," I replied. "I believe it was inevitable."

"I agree."

She just seemed very sad. It was hard not to get dragged down by the depressed mood. It was as if she had no hope left.

"Sarenah didn't recognize you?" She looked back to the open windows. I followed her gaze. No one was there. I was sure that Rebecca had every right to be paranoid, though. This entire place Rebecca was

241

now living in gave me the creeps. A luxury hotel suite in Hell didn't sit well in my stomach.

"She had no remembrance of me, no."

Rebecca sat there silent for what seemed like a very long time. "That's the reason I've been forced to remain here."

"Rebecca, I'm sorry. I don't understand."

"The memories, Cynda. Don't you see? They erased everyone's memories of what happened. They sent you to Earth alone and knew you wouldn't speak a word of it to anyone. They tried to erase mine as well, but they couldn't. It seems as though it's impossible for anyone to get inside my head."

"Of course it is."

She looked up at me then, her eyes questioning my statement. "What do you mean?"

"You're a witch in yourself, just a different kind."

"What?" Rebecca asked, her eyes full of fear and doubt.

"You've never known what you are?" I asked her. "What you're capable of?"

"I tagged along with Sarenah when she was studying with you. I learned a few things here and

242

there. I know I stopped you from turning the town and all its people into ash that night, but I gave it all up. I wanted nothing more to do with any of it." She seemed angry that I had suggested she was a witch.

I blinked a few times, my swollen eye tearing up from the damage the demon had done to me. "You read my books. You mastered something incredibly difficult, some even think impossible. Rebecca, you're an obstructer."

"A what?"

I small smile crossed my lips. "An obstructer. I'm almost positive everyone else knows what you are. I just can't believe *you* didn't. You don't cast spells, you put an end to them. They couldn't take your memories from you because you stopped it from happening. You studied it in my books, but it's your gift, Rebecca. I thought you had embraced it. I never knew you didn't really know what you were doing. You're very powerful to have stopped me that night. I was determined to kill them all."

Rebecca stood then, angry. "I wanted your sisters dead! They were terrible, mean people!" She was yelling now. So much for being discrete. "I only saved you because you helped Sarenah, and I..." She covered her face with her hands as she broke down in tears and fell to her knees. "I love my sister!"

I wrapped my arms around her and held the girl and just let her sob. I was sure it had been a long time since she'd had a good cry, and she needed to get it all out. I had just informed her that she was an obstructer, and it obviously wasn't sitting well with her right now, either.

"You're strong and powerful. They couldn't take your memories, and you need to focus on how strong you are. You've survived this whole thing. We all have," I told her, hoping the words would soothe her.

"But now what?" she asked, the sobs beginning to cease now. "How will we survive it a second time?"

I didn't know how to answer her. I wasn't sure we would survive. I knew that Rebecca and I were being used as tools to try to put an end to a cycle which had a force behind it completely unknown to all elements at hand. They thought the two of us may have a clue, even when we really didn't. They were going to try to use us to their advantage to break the cycle from occurring again. I didn't want to die.

Would I be able to save us all? Did I want to anymore? Perhaps there should be an end to this. If I was able to stop it, I would be able to save myself in the process and they'd never have a reason to come after me again.

21

Sarenah

I was shackled to a wall in the darkness, my arms and legs bound so tight I couldn't move.

"Wait here," the hellhound had told me.

I was separated from Saint and Tabian. We were all awaiting our end. This was it. Soon I'd be feeling pain I was sure would be so unbearable I wished I would die, and then after they were content with tormenting me, I *would* die. I wasn't even sure what happened to an angel when they died. Would I simply vanish?

My heart ached. Had this all been for nothing? I came on an impulse, one with such force and power it's all I thought about until I finally gave in and went for it. And now, not only had I gotten myself into a mess, one that was inescapable, but Saint and Tabian as well. What a terrible creature I was. How could I be so selfish to let them come with me? I should've insisted on going alone. If my hands were free right now I'd be pounding my fists into the rocks out of frustration about my own idiocy.

A single tear slipped down my cheek. I never cried, but the helpless feeling was beginning to shake me. The elements of good and evil, those in between...I had never felt like I had fit in. And the only thing that ever made sense to me – Draco – even he was something that was confusing. I couldn't even reach him to try to make sense of it all. My head drooped as the heaviness that was my failure took over, and I wallowed in it.

Oh, Draco, I have failed us both.

I allowed my eyes to go shut. There was no fight left in me.

Sarenah, why do you come to me like this? Where are you? Are you okay?

He was speaking to me again. I couldn't express how grateful I was to hear his sultry voice.

I can't find you. I tried to fight them like you said, but there's too many.

I don't understand. You're not in Hell, are you?

I am.

There was a long, silent pause before he spoke again. *Why would you come? I'm nothing.*

You're wrong. You're everything. It doesn't matter now.

It matters to me. I'm locked away. I can't get out.

My heart sank. *Was it because of me?*

248

It was because of us.

Someone is trying to hide something from us.

I think you're right.

And still I struggled with the notion that we could speak to each other. *What's this connection we have? How can I hear you?*

It's just as odd to me as it is to you, yet comforting. Please, don't stop. Tell me everything about yourself.

I'm an angel who puts her trust in a very dangerous creature.

What a cliché we've become.

I almost wanted to laugh aloud.

Sarenah...

I'm here.

Evil creatures like me are incapable of feeling anything, yet here I am pouring out my heart to you. It shouldn't be this easy to feel.

I know exactly what you mean.

I only touched you that one time, and it was the only time I've ever felt anything...ever.

It was impulsive and very uncharacteristic of me.

249

It was magnificent. And then you ran off, and I didn't even know who you were until I got locked away.

I'm sorry. I didn't want to tell you. I was afraid...

Sarenah...I understand why you didn't tell me. It wouldn't have made a difference, though. It's not making one now.

Draco...I don't want to die.

You're not. Sit tight. Stall. Do whatever it takes to buy me a little more time. You trust me, right?

You know I do.

Then think about that moment we shared when we ran into each other's arms without any remorse. Trust in my words.

I'm listening.

Run fast, run furious to the arms you trust the most and hold you tightest.

I sucked in a deep breath of air. I would run straight into his arms the moment I saw him again. *Draco, what are you planning to do?*

Start a war in Hell.

22

Cynda

"Well, it looks like our precious princess *is* able to speak after all this time."

Rebecca and I looked up simultaneously as a demon disguised as a very attractive man approached us. It made me wonder what poor soul he was pretending to be. His wavy, dark blonde hair stopped at the nape of his neck.

He smiled. "It looks like the two of you have had a nice chat. I hope you've been able to use your time wisely, to sort some things out."

Rebecca's eyes returned to their saddened state. She looked away from him and folded her hands across her lap as she sat.

He pointed at me. "You, come with me."

I hesitated a moment, looking back at a girl that had been my friend lifetimes ago.

"Now," he added.

Sighing, I walked out of the glass doors and back into another furnished open room. "Please, sit," he said, gesturing toward an orange-colored couch. I watched him sit across from me on a chair, the smile still on his lips. "So, tell me, what have you figured out about our little situation?"

"I wouldn't call it little," I mumbled before realizing I had spoken without thinking again. I looked up, waiting for that look of fury that everyone down here seemed to have, and was surprised when it didn't come. He chuckled.

"No, no, you're right. It's not exactly a little problem, is it? It's probably the biggest problem we've ever faced, and we're all in it together, aren't we?" The voice didn't match the physique. He was way too high-pitched, too whiney.

"Who are you?" I asked, my curiosity getting the best of me.

He placed a finger to his mouth. "You may call me Eric."

"No, I didn't mean your name. Like, what is your rank?"

"Does that really concern you, my little witch? I mean, all of us down here are truly evil. Is one of us worse than the other?"

I frowned. *Good point, Eric, but somehow it seems to me like I'm actually talking with someone intelligent, someone higher up than even the counselors, someone who can actually control their*

253

temper. "Rebecca knows her power now. I had to be the one to tell her about it."

"Yes, yes, obstructer. She's a very rare creature indeed." He had a smooth way of speaking, almost snake-like when the words were pressed off his tongue. His eyes never left me.

"You brought me here to help stop all of this, yet I feel like I'm not getting anything in return," I stated boldly.

He narrowed his eyes at me. "What is it you want? What is it you would like to know?"

"Rebecca...why is she here? Why wasn't she taken to Heaven? It looks like she's protected here, trapped, yet protected. I'm just trying to understand the reasoning behind her captivity. Obviously there's the memory aspect, but there seems like there's something more to it."

He continued to stare at me, his eyes seeming to get shades darker as he wet his dry lips with his tongue before speaking. "They didn't know what to do with her because of not being able to rid her of the memories."

"They?"

He looked annoyed that I didn't know. "Heaven," he hissed out as if it was such a hindrance to say. "They wanted her. She has so much good radiating in her, but the obstructer part of her...it was too risky for her to be released. We settled on arrangements, those very arrangements you see before you today."

"And no one can harm her?"

He eyed me cautiously for a moment. "Correct. She is protected by the Light."

"Does Rebecca know that?" I asked a little too quickly.

A smile returned to his face. "No, I don't believe she does. We have to keep her in her place, after all, don't we?" He leaned forward. "Now, enough with all these questions. What do we do about Draco?"

It was hard for me to look at the black spaces that should be his eyes without cowering, but I somehow managed to keep it together. I took a deep breath as I thought about the entire situation for a moment. The key was getting rid of Draco entirely, but how? It seemed impossible. They thought Rebecca was powerful with being an obstructer. They must have also thought I was powerful or they wouldn't have forced me to be here.

They were going to kill me one way or another, whether I cooperated or not. This I was sure of. There was no way I was getting released this time around. It was hard for me to wrap my mind around the fact that this all seemed to be weighing on my shoulders all of a sudden, as if my intelligence and power could rid the world and both Heaven and Hell of Draco. I hadn't performed the spell, Sarenah had, and yet there had been no mention of her while I was here.

Since I was sure I was dead either way, I had a decision to make. Would everyone be better off if Draco was destroyed? He had turned everyone's lives upside down, yet it wasn't his fault, was it?

I had to do what I thought was best. Rebecca wanted him gone, and I highly valued her opinion. As I contemplated it all again and again in my mind, Eric simply watched me with no sign of emotion on his face. He was an intimidating creature, yes, but I held all the power. I wasn't sure if I was making the right choice, but it had been decided.

"Well, I think the information you've given me has proven useful," I commented.

Now he looked interested. "Do tell, witch." He leaned back in his chair as if relaxed again while crossing his legs.

"Rebecca is protected by the Light. That means no one belonging to Hell can harm her, correct?"

He nodded. "That's right."

"Does Draco fall under that category?"

Eric looked a little puzzled as he raised his eyebrows.

"Does Draco truly belong to Hell?"

He stared at me for a moment thinking over what I had said. "You know, witch, now that you mention it, I'm not so sure he does." He smiled. "I think I like what you're getting at."

Now it was my turn to smirk. "Am I granted my freedom to return to Earth if I formulate a plan to destroy Draco?"

"Of course," Eric replied. "You have my word." His eyes seemed to gleam as he said it.

Yeah, right, I thought. "I believe Rebecca is your key then." My stomach twisted in knots. There was no

257

going back now. I had already said too much. "Where is Draco?"

"Somewhere…very dark." Another gleam emanated from his eyes.

"We take Rebecca to him. I'm sure he's bloodthirsty. He won't even know who she is. He has no memories, I'm guessing, right?"

Eric nodded. "He does not."

"So I'm certain he'll kill her."

"And then?" he asked.

"And then Heaven will be so angry that one of their protected has been murdered that they will surely lash out and either destroy him themselves or hand him over to you so that he does truly belong to Hell."

He thought it over for a minute, his finger back to his lips. "And you would be willing to sacrifice the obstructer?"

I shrugged. "I am a witch, aren't I? Call me selfish, but I'd like to be the one walking out of here alive."

A smile formed on his face again. "You're a little devil, aren't you witch?"

I didn't know if I liked his choice of words, but I forced a small laugh.

"This plan of yours is worth a shot. It's the best I've heard so far, so let's go with it. I would love to get rid of Rebecca and Draco at the same time. She has been a burden to me as she's been so...protected." He glared at me, his face stern. "Now go and do whatever it takes to convince Rebecca she must go see Draco, and make it sound urgent. We're running out of time."

I stood and walked back to Rebecca's room. Eric had already opened the glass doors and was waiting for me. As I entered, he closed the door behind me. I looked back, but he had disappeared.

I rushed over to her side and kneeled down on the floor. "Rebecca..."

"I saw you talking to him. Nothing good can come out of talking to *him,*"she whispered.

"Listen to me very carefully. I have to say this quietly. I can't risk him hearing."

She didn't look my way.

"He wants you to go to Draco."

"No," Rebecca said.

"No? Rebecca, listen to me."

"I don't want Draco to live. He shouldn't be alive right now."

I nodded my head. "I agree with you. I have a plan. Just hear me out. He thinks by your going to see Draco, that in turn Draco will kill you. You've been protected by Heaven the whole time you've been here. Did you even know that, Rebecca? You've been protected, and if Draco kills you, he'll be damned to Hell forever, but that's not what's going to happen."

Tears filled her eyes. "How did this all happen, Cynda? Do you even know?"

I shook my head. "No, I don't. Please listen to me. You have so much power within you. I'll do a spell and feed off your obstructer energy. Together I think it'll be enough to kill Draco. I just need you to keep him distracted long enough for me to mumble the spell."

"Okay," she whispered. "You'll kill him?"

I nodded. "I won't let anything happen to you."

"When do we go?" she asked.

I looked toward the glass doors. Eric had reappeared. "Now."

Rebecca took my hand as we walked out. I could feel the wrinkles creasing my forehead as the worry set in. Had I just backstabbed the only truly good person I had ever known?

23

Draco

Footsteps echoed down the corridor. Another visitor. Someone else for me to take my fury out on.

I didn't move as the footsteps grew closer to my cell. Another lantern was held up, the glow bright as I shielded my eyes and squinted to see who it was. A counselor.

"Draco," he acknowledged me.

He'd probably be too smart to get too close. I decided not to stand or show any respect for his presence. "What do you want?" I snapped at him.

"I've come to help you."

"Help is not something given without a price."

He paused for a moment before continuing. "I may get in trouble for coming here, but someone needed to warn you."

"About what?"

"Listen very carefully to my instructions. There is a young woman coming to see you soon. When she does, you must kill her. Do not hesitate. Kill her," he said.

I rubbed the sharp stubble on my cheeks. "And why would I do that?"

263

"Because it's a test, Draco. If you fail, you'll never get out of here."

I fought hard at the anger rising within me. Test after test is all I had passed until I had become a great leader of the dark army. I had still ended up here, locked away, feeling as though I were losing my sanity bit by bit like some sort of worthless animal. No. Everyone was for themselves. The moment you thought you had a friend was the moment you should be afraid that you had let someone get too close. That this counselor was trying to make a fool out of me only made the craziness stirring within want some sort of release. I did need a kill, but it wouldn't be some girl. It would be this foul creature standing on the other side of those bars and anyone else that would try to cross me.

"You're helping me, why?" My senses felt as if they were on fire, every ounce of me about to burst. Who was this so-called girl that was being brought to me, and what was her significance? Something was being plotted against me, I just wish I knew what. They had had all this time to torture me, and no physical torment had even been made. Mentally, yes, that was working against me, but if I didn't totally lose grasp with reality, what was the reason I was being held like this? I had seen soul after soul begging for someone to help them as they burned in the flames. Hell was all about pain, yet none had been inflicted upon me. My mind was racing right along with my heart. Why not just kill me and get it over with?

"I want to see you back on our side," he whispered.

Draco...please hurry.

Sarenah's voice. I had to go to her. I wanted to roar out my frustration, the heat within me not abating.

What had he meant by back on their side? I had never left their side. "Who is this girl..." Before I could finish, the glow of another light caught my attention. Someone else was approaching. I focused on it as the light grew brighter with each step they made.

Something was happening...something very wrong. Maybe this was it. This *girl* who was coming to see me was linked to my demise, but I wouldn't die, not until I knew Sarenah was safe. I had promised her I'd come for her. *Just open that damn door a little notch so I can kill you all,* I thought.

"Draco," the counselor hissed. "Remember my instructions!"

I narrowed my eyes as two faces came into view until they were both standing in front of the locked door. One was an older woman with short hair. Her eyes were locked on me as she held the hand of a much younger woman by her side who had long blonde hair and tears in her eyes. I studied these women in curiosity. They didn't look like they belonged here. Beyond their physical appearance of weakness, their eyes lacked a certain smugness that was always seen in demons. These women looked sad and almost fearful as they stood there peering in at me.

Draco...

I stiffened as I grasped the bars with my fingers. Right now, I needed to try to shake Sarenah from my head. I couldn't tell her the horrible thoughts of dread running through my mind. She was already discouraged as it was. I refused to add to her burden.

"Who are you?" I asked, alarmed at how calm my own voice sounded in comparison to mere moments ago.

The blonde's eyes had shifted to the floor. She looked up at me then, her eyes full of hatred and fear. Tears began to stream down her cheeks. "I'm Rebecca. I've come to give you a message."

24

Cynda

I couldn't believe it. Draco. Here he was after all this time. They had put him in captivity like an animal. I withheld from laughing aloud at the similarities. He may as well be labeled an animal...a monster was more like it.

It had been centuries since I had looked upon this sweet, yet horrific face. He was as magnificent now as he had been back then. He was still built strong, his hair a little longer maybe and circles under his eyes, but still astonishing nevertheless. I wasn't told that he was detained, but I knew immediately that it had to have been because of Sarenah. They had been afraid knowing those two had crossed paths, and rightly so. My eyes moved to the bars. *Really? This has held him in?* If only Draco knew what he was truly capable of. I wanted to smile. Things were about to change. I had no idea if I was making the right decision, but I knew one thing for sure: I was here to change the plans of everyone involved. The past that everyone was feverishly attempting to stop from repeating itself was going to come to full sequence tonight. I was bursting at the seams at the excitement of it all. I had been witness to it all those

269

years ago. I just hoped no one would catch on and put an end to me before I got to see the show.

I looked back at the counselor, my stomach twisting in knots as I hoped Rebecca would follow through.

"You have to keep him calm, Rebecca," I instructed her as we had walked down here. "Just comfort him in any way. You can't let him get in a rage."

"You'll do the spell?" Rebecca had asked.

"I told you I won't fail you, and I mean it."

I don't think I could've stressed the comfort part any more. It was up to fate, but I so very much hoped fate was on my side. There was nothing more exciting than the anticipation of it all.

The counselor pushed in front of us, his fingers working the lock. I thought Draco might try to escape, but he didn't. He actually took a few steps backward.

Okay, I thought. *First dilemma avoided. Good boy on staying put, Draco.*

"Go," the counselor said sternly.

Rebecca glanced back at me. I nodded my head at her, giving her that extra reassurance. She had always been ¹ afraid of Draco and now was no exception, but her desire to save Sarenah was more powerful than her fear. I watched her go inside as the counselor slammed the door shut and quickly locked it again. The loud bang from the metal door colliding with other metal echoed down the corridor.

I felt a familiar arrogance taking over me, one similar to when I had almost been burned at the stake. Then I had held all the power with my spell. Now I had the power of knowledge, the only one who knew how this was all supposed to play out.

I'm so very sorry, Rebecca, dear. There will be no spells attempted this time.

I kept careful watch as my stunning Rebecca puppet stood there hesitantly for a few seconds before approaching Draco. Neither one of them knew what to make of the other. It was beautiful. I wanted to fall back and recline in a comfy chair at a theater, a box of popcorn in my hands.

I could see her lips moving. Darn, I wish I could hear it! I crossed my arms. Draco was saying

271

something back to her now. I flicked another piece of imaginary popcorn in my mouth, wary that the counselor had his eyes glued to the same scene.

I unfolded my arms and began fidgeting with my bottom lip. Rebecca was close to him now. She was whispering. *Comfort,* I repeated. *Comfort him.* And then I froze as it happened. Rebecca placed her hand on his arm to comfort him. *Good girl, Rebecca! Good girl!*

Draco jerked his arm away from her. He had that look on his face again, one full of such intensity. I braced myself for what was to come next.

Draco's face twisted as he winced from the pain. It had been so long since they had erased his memories. His poor body probably didn't know what to make of what was firing off in his brain. His legs buckled as he went down to his knees, his fingers scratching at his neck as he writhed from the pain.

Rebecca looked over at me. She, too, knew what was happening. Our eyes met. She now knew my lies. I wasn't standing here in deep concentration on a spell. I was giving the unnatural elements back what belonged to them. Rebecca hurried over to the edge of the cell. I would've backed up too, but there was nowhere to go. A wall was right behind me.

The veins in Draco's neck bulged along with his eyes. He was gasping for air as small pulsations of smoke exited his mouth. He tried to cough, but couldn't. His entire body jerked backward in one swift movement. I cringed as it looked like his spine had just snapped in two. He then flailed forward into a huddled ball on the floor before swinging his arms back, the monster within him now bursting to life.

The ceiling, composed of rock, busted with Draco's head, the pieces raining down around us. Rebecca cried out as Draco's side exploded to full growth, almost smashing her in the process. The metal fell away as if paper to him now. Rebecca rushed behind me. I was sure she was probably pinning herself against the wall, but I couldn't move. I didn't want to take my eyes off him as the walls crumbled around us. Rebecca had given Draco the extra push he needed. Draco was now fully transformed into a dragon.

The details all came flooding back to me just as they had hundreds of years ago. He was a massive, majestic creature of shimmering black, outlined in a red hue. As he tossed his head back angrily, his dark mane with traces of red fell around his wings. His eyes were glowing and fierce as smoke now poured out of his snout. He was magnificent. He was one of a kind and would now tear Hell apart piece by piece.

"What have you done, Cynda?" Rebecca cried out.

I had lost track of the counselor. I turned to get a better look at where he had gone when I felt an object being pushed through the skin of my stomach. I buckled over, my hands now grasping onto a sword I was sure had gone completely through me and out my back. I looked down at my blood-covered hands and tried to yank the blade from my body, but it was no use. My strength was leaving me. The counselor glared at me. I had been disobedient to Hell's wishes. I had fooled them into believing I would help them. My punishment was death, and I knew it would come swiftly.

It didn't matter now as a strange fog began to settle in around me. I had made the right choice, I was sure. Draco was now free to fight his own battles raging within himself.

A smile played on my lips as the arrogance returned with the knowledge of what I had done. Rebecca was an obstructer. She could block certain things, other times harvest them. She didn't know the extent of her power. All it took was a single exchange of touch from her to Draco for her to give him every single one of his memories back. It had caused him pain, I knew, as each memory had attached with it the most powerful emotion there is. Draco now remembered the unconditional love that he had for Sarenah.

25

Draco

My head kept crashing into rock which made my irritation grow, if that was even possible. What the hell had just happened? I was still trying to wrap my mind around the fact that I had just burst forth into a huge dragon, my body clumsy as I tried to maneuver it in such a tight space. Flames were dancing off my tongue with each breath. What had that girl done to me? Her touch had been so...excruciatingly painful. And then my head started to kill me like someone was pressing on both sides of my skull as if to crush it.

I squinted my eyes, and it was as if I could zoom in my vision. I looked at Rebecca and Cynda.

Rebecca and Cynda?

How the hell did I know their names?

And then I remembered...Cynda was a witch and longtime friend. Her loyalties knew no bounds. Rebecca was Sarenah's younger sister. The memories were flooding my brain now. I remembered it all. Rebecca's touch had released me from the grasps of my forced amnesia.

Cynda fell to the ground and flopped onto her side. I could see the sword protruding all the way through and out her back. She was dead.

Anger burned through me. Without hesitation, something triggered in my mind, and a fireball exploded into the counselor who had been trying to get away. He shrieked out in surprise as he dissipated into nothing. Cynda was gone. She had helped me. I didn't know how, but I was sure of it.

It seems as if my time is up. What I wouldn't have given to feel your touch just one last time...

Sarenah. This time it hit me with such force I almost stumbled back, but I stood solid now on four legs instead of two. The thought that she was in any kind of danger made me go ballistic. Sarenah and I, our undeniable love for one another, was the reason all of this had happened. I didn't belong to Hell. She didn't belong to Heaven. We simply belonged to each other. The elements in the universe had been trying to contain me by keeping us apart, by making us forget. The knowledge that we had just spent hundreds of years without each other against our will made even more fire spit from my throat.

I looked at Rebecca. I bent my neck down for her to get on. She hesitated and glanced down at Cynda's lifeless body. The moment I knew she was secure on

278

my back, I began breaking down every particle of Hell in front of me to get to where they were keeping Sarenah.

26

Sarenah

The hellhounds had commanded we be dragged to some sort of fiery pits. They had me by the hair with their teeth. Without the use of my hands and feet, there was nothing else I could do but endure this pain and humiliation. Saint and Tabian were being dragged by their feet, their torsos being forced over the jagged ground.

There was no need to be a sobbing mess now. I was going to hold it together and not regret the choices I had recently made. I was going to be strong and face whatever destiny death held for me. I wouldn't beg for my life. It would be of no use anyway, but I wouldn't dare give them the satisfaction of knowing they broke me.

A hideous roar bellowed out. I felt the hellhound release his grasp on my hair. I managed to pull myself into a seated position. Saint and Tabian were nearby. We exchanged glances. The last terrible noise we had heard had come from the hellhounds. Whatever this was, they didn't seem to recognize it. They looked shaken up.

I had to turn my head as debris from the ceiling and surrounding walls fell, creating a massive cloud of dust which made us all cough. I attempted to open my eyes again. I could taste tiny particles of rock on my tongue. I gasped.

Staring back at me were fiery red eyes. As the dust settled more, the huge form of a dragon was merely inches away from my face. I chastised myself for showing the fear that I knew was written all over my expression right now, but I had never seen such a magnificent and frightening creature before. He was massive. I gulped for a breath of air as my heart pumped wildly within my chest.

A sudden pain began stinging right behind my wing. I winced as it felt like someone had taken a hot piece of steel and pressed it into my back.

Miss me?

My eyes grew even larger.

Draco? Draco, where are you? There's a hideous dragon in front of me!

Hey, now, watch what you say. That hideous part hurts my feelings.

I stared into his eyes, his nostrils with smoke pouring from them.

Draco...you're a...dragon?

Are you hurt?

There was just that weird sensation of burning in my back, but I could manage through it. *No.*

Draco's head went back as a flame burst out of his mouth. It landed on one of the hellhounds who began screaming, its body on fire.

"Release them!" a demon shouted out.

I looked around then. We were completely surrounded by evil creatures of all different ranks. All these disgusting, evil creatures were watching us, their underworld barely able to hold itself up from Draco's enormous body slamming into it. There was this stunning dragon towering above them all. All eyes were glued on him. What was Draco's next action? No one moved.

"Do it!" another one hollered.

They're afraid of you.

I thought I saw amusement dance in his eyes. *Petrified.*

A few brave creatures clambered to get to where we were. They hastily cut the ropes from my arms and legs and did the same for Saint and Tabian, their eyes still on Draco. If demons quaked in fear, they were all doing it now.

Get on, tell Saint and Tabian to do the same.

I looked over at my friends. "He wants us to get on his back."

Saint gave me a look like I was insane. "What? You mean the dragon?"

Draco turned to his side, revealing a beautiful blonde girl straddling his neck. I didn't have time to question who she was, although a pang of jealousy ripped through me.

"Yes," I replied. "The dragon is Draco." I got to my feet and allowed my hand to skim over the smooth black skin of Draco's neck.

I may need a massage later.

I burst out laughing. The demons didn't seem pleased. I got on his neck behind the girl. I then held out my hand for Saint and Tabian who, although hesitant, decided to trust my action as safe.

It was such a peculiar feeling being perched on top of such a creature. It felt empowering. A million questions darted through my mind, but I tried to block them out. I savored this moment. The dragon was saving the angel. He was saving us all.

"Open up a portal to Earth!" someone yelled from below. "Hurry!"

My hands grasped around Draco's thick mane as his head collided with part of the ceiling overhead. Boulders broke away, crushing demons below. A black hole formed above our heads, a portal.

"Sarenah?" Saint said.

"Yeah?"

"How did you get this tattoo on your back?" he asked.

"Tattoo? Saint, I don't have a tattoo." He was now touching the area on my back that had felt like it was on fire. The memory of being in Draco's arms came flooding back. I had felt the burning pain then, too.

"Um, yes, you do."

"What is it?"

"It's a picture of two dragons."

I could hear Draco chuckling to himself in my head. What did he know that I didn't?

The portal grew larger. The blonde girl turned around to look at me.

"Hello, sister."

"Sister?" I asked.

She rolled her eyes and then turned just enough so that her hand was now resting on mine. I felt a sudden rush enter my head. It was like a blinding white blur that made me both dizzy and nauseated.

"Help hold her up," I heard the girl say as Saint wrapped his arms around my waist to prevent me from falling.

What happened? You okay?

I sucked in a few breaths of air as I tried to steady myself. The fog was lifting from my mind. Oh, Draco...

What? What is it?

Draco, I remember everything.

Epilogue

The elements had miscalculated the sequence of events. They had tried to keep us all away from each other, stole our memories and tried to do everything in their power to prevent it from happening again.

A dragon was considered unnatural. The concept of the creature had been merely figments of the imagination until Draco. He was the only one, and he was insanely in love with me, and I with him. We were bound together now, our bond unbreakable. They had failed at what they had attempted to do. The elements of the universe were working together for the very first time to get Draco's immense power under control. He was created with neither good nor evil. It wasn't even known if he had a soul, but he had a heart, and that heart belonged only to me.

Now both sides - good, evil, and that in between, who belonged to Earth, were fearful of what this could mean for the future. Evil was surpassing its boundaries to attack Heaven, each of them casting the blame upon the other for upsetting Draco, and in turn, him becoming a dragon once again after having centuries of peace. Draco's temper was of utmost concern. When he was in dragon form, there was no telling what may happen. However, I remained calm. My heart was filled with bliss as I now clung to the memories. We wouldn't let anyone steal them from us again. The war between good and evil was raging around us, but our own war against them, our vengeance, was brewing within.

The adventure has only begun...

Authors note and Information

Dear reader,

We hope that you have enjoyed Evanescent and are excited to continue the journey with Sarenah, Draco, and their friends as well as their enemies.

If you enjoyed this book, we would appreciate it if you would leave just a short review on Amazon.

Reviews are very important.

Thank you!

Sara & Wendy

https://www.facebook.com/sempiternalfans
https://www.facebook.com/SaraVZook
https://www.facebook.com/SaraVZook
https://www.facebook.com/PlanettopiaPublishing
https://www.twitter.com/SaraVZook
https://twitter.com/WSChartier
http://the-sempiternal-series.tumblr.com/